The
White Horse
of Zennor
and other stories

MICHAEL MORPURGO

EGMONT

EGMONT

We bring stories to life

For Ted and Carol

First published in Great Britain in 1982
by Kaye & Ward Ltd
This edition published 2011
by Egmont UK Limited
239 Kensington High Street, London W8 6SA

Text copyright © 1982 Michael Morpurgo
Cover photography © Shutterstock
The moral rights of the author have been asserted

ISBN 978 1 4052 5675 9

1 3 5 7 9 10 8 6 4 2

www.egmont.co.uk
www.michaelmorpurgo.org

A CIP catalogue record for this title is available from the British Library

Typeset by Avon Dataset Ltd, Bidford on Avon, Warwickshire
Printed and bound in Great Britain by the CPI Group

MIX
Paper
FSC FSC® C018306

INTRODUCTION

ONE OF THE LAST PLACES YOU COME TO before Cornwall disappears into the Atlantic Ocean is the tiny churchtown of Zennor. Since the beginning of time, strange and mysterious things have happened here. There are stories from the past of mermaids and spriggans and knockers and witches. The stories in this book however do not come from the past. They have all happened in my lifetime.

The 'Eagle's Nest' of the title is the great outcrop of rock that dominates the fields and farmsteads below. From here you can see the coastline all the way from St Ives to Pendeen Lighthouse. You can see the churchtown of Zennor itself below the high moor, and you can feel that here anything is possible, perhaps even probable.

Before you begin 'The Giant's Necklace' I would ask you to read the stories in the order in which you find them. You will understand why when you have finished the book.

M. M. Zennor 1982

CONTENTS

For Ted and Carol

THE GIANT'S NECKLACE

So, a mining story to start with. For many years I used to go every summer to Zennor. I read Cornish legends pastries *, researched the often tragic history of tin mining in Penrith, wandered the wild moors above Zennor Churchtown. I wrote a book of five short stories called* The White Horse of Zennor. *This is the first.*

The necklace stretched from one end of the kitchen table to the other, around the sugar bowl at the far end and back again, stopping only a few inches short of the toaster. The discovery on the beach of a length of abandoned fishing line draped with seaweed had first suggested the idea to Cherry; and every day of the holiday since then had been spent in one single-minded pursuit, the creation of a necklace of glistening pink cowrie shells. She had sworn to herself and to everyone else that the necklace would not be complete until it reached the toaster; and when Cherry vowed she would do something, she invariably did it.

Cherry was the youngest in a family of older brothers, four of them, who had teased her relentlessly since the day she was born, eleven years before. She referred to them as 'the four mistakes', for it was a family joke that each son had been an attempt to produce a daughter. To their huge delight Cherry reacted passionately to any slight or insult whether intended or not. Their particular targets were her size, which was diminutive compared with theirs, and her dark flashing eyes that could wither with one scornful look, her 'zapping' look, they called it. Although the teasing was interminable it was rarely hurtful, nor was it intended to be, for her brothers adored her; and she knew it.

Cherry was poring over her necklace, still in her dressing gown. Breakfast had just been cleared away and she was alone with her mother. She fingered the shells lightly, turning them gently until the entire necklace lay flat with the rounded pink of the shells all uppermost. Then she bent down and breathed on each of them in turn, polishing them carefully with a napkin.

'There's still the sea in them,' she said to no one in particular. 'You can still smell it, and I washed them and washed them, you know.'

'You've only got today, Cherry,' said her mother coming over to the table and putting an arm round her. 'Just today, that's all. We're off back home tomorrow morning first thing. Why don't you call it a day, dear? You've been at it every day – you *must* be tired of it by now. There's no need to go on, you know. We all think it's a fine necklace and quite long enough. It's long enough surely?'

Cherry shook her head slowly. 'No,' she said. 'Only that little bit left to do and then it'll be finished.'

'But they'll take hours to collect, dear,' her mother

said weakly, recognising and at the same time respecting her daughter's persistence.

'Only a few hours,' said Cherry, bending over, her brows furrowing critically as she inspected a flaw in one of her shells, 'that's all it'll take. D'you know, there are five thousand, three hundred and twenty-five shells in my necklace already? I counted them, so I know.'

'Isn't that enough, Cherry?' her mother said desperately.

'No,' said Cherry. 'I said I'd reach the toaster, and I'm going to reach the toaster.'

Her mother turned away to continue the drying-up.

'Well, I can't spend all day on the beach today, Cherry,' she said. 'If you haven't finished by the time we come away, I'll have to leave you there. We've got to pack up and tidy the house – there'll be no time in the morning.'

'I'll be all right,' said Cherry, cocking her head on one side to view the necklace from a different angle. 'There's never been a necklace like this before, not in all the world. I'm sure there hasn't.' And then, 'You can leave me there, Mum, and I'll walk back. It's only a mile or so along the cliff path and half a mile back across the fields. I've done it before on my own. It's not far.'

There was a thundering on the stairs and a sudden rude invasion of the kitchen. Cherry was surrounded by her four brothers who leant over the table in mock appreciation of her necklace.

'Ooh, pretty.'

'Do they come in other colours? I mean, pink's not my colour.'

'Who's it for? An elephant?'

'It's for a giant,' said Cherry. 'It's a giant's necklace, and it's still not big enough.'

It was the perfect answer, an answer she knew would send her brothers into fits of laughter. She loved to make them laugh at her and could do it at the drop of a hat. Of course she no more believed in giants than they did, but if it tickled them pink to believe she did, then why not pretend?

She turned on them, fists flailing and chased them back up the stairs, her eyes burning with simulated fury. 'Just 'cos you don't believe in anything 'cept motorbikes and football and all that rubbish, just 'cos you're great big, fat, ignorant pigs . . .' She hurled insults up the stairs, and the worse the insult the more they loved it.

Boat Cove just below Zennor Head was the beach they had found and occupied. Every year for as long as Cherry could remember they had rented the same granite cottage, set back in the fields below the Eagle's Nest and every year they came to the same beach because no one else did. In two weeks not another soul had ventured down the winding track through the bracken from the coastal path. It was a long climb down and a very much longer one up. The beach itself was almost hidden from the path that ran along the cliff top a hundred feet above. It was private and perfect and theirs. The boys swam in amongst the rocks, diving and snorkelling for hours on end. Her mother and father would sit side by side on stripey deck chairs. She would read endlessly and he would close his eyes against the sun and dream for hours on end.

Cherry moved away from them and clambered over the rocks to a narrow strip of sand in the cove beyond the rocks, and here it was that she mined for the cowrie shells. In the gritty sand under the cliff face she had found a particularly rich deposit. She was looking for pink cowrie shells of a uniform length, colour and shape – that was what took the time. Occasionally the boys would swim around the rocks and in to her little beach, emerging from the sea all goggled and flippered to mock her. But as she paid them little attention they soon tired and went away again. She knew time was running short. This was her very last chance to find enough shells to complete the giant's necklace, and it had to be done.

The sea was calmer that day than she had ever seen it. The heat beat down from a windless, cloudless sky; even the gulls and kittiwakes seemed to be silenced by the sun. Cherry searched on, stopping only for a picnic lunch of pasties and tomatoes with the family before returning at once to her shells.

In the end the heat proved too much for her mother and father, who left the beach earlier than usual in mid-afternoon to begin to tidy up the cottage. The boys soon followed because they had tired of finding miniature crabs and seaweed instead of the sunken wrecks and treasure they had been seeking. So, by tea-time Cherry was left on her own on the beach with strict instructions to keep her hat on, not to bathe alone and to be back well before dark. She had calculated she needed one hundred and fifty more cowrie shells and so far she had only found eighty. She would be back, she insisted, when she had finished collecting enough shells and not before.

Had she not been so immersed in her search, sifting the shells through her fingers, she would have noticed the dark grey bank of cloud rolling in from the Atlantic. She would have noticed the white horses gathering out at sea and the tide moving remorselessly in to cover the rocks between her and Boat Cove. When the clouds cut off the warmth from the sun as evening came on and the sea turned grey, she shivered with cold and put on her sweater and jeans. She did look up then and saw the angry sea, but she saw no threat in that and did not look back over her shoulder to Boat Cove. She was aware that time was running out so she went down on her knees again and dug feverishly in the sand. She had to collect thirty more shells.

It was the baleful sound of the foghorn somewhere out at sea beyond Gunnards Head that at last forced Cherry to take some account of the incoming tide. She looked for the rocks she would have to clamber over to reach Boat Cove again and the winding track that would take her up to the cliff path and safety, but they were gone. Where they should have been, the sea was already driving in against the cliff face. She was cut off. In a confusion of wonder and fear she looked out to sea at the heaving ocean that moved in towards her, seeing it now as a writhing grey monster breathing its fury on the rocks with every pounding wave.

Still Cherry did not forget her shells, but wrapping them inside her towel she tucked them into her sweater and waded out through the surf towards the rocks. If she timed it right, she reasoned, she could scramble back over them and into the Cove as the surf retreated. She reached the first of the rocks without too much difficulty; the sea here seemed to be protected from the force of the ocean by the rocks further out. Holding fast to the first rock she came to and with the sea up around her waist, she waited for the next incoming wave to break and retreat. The wave was unexpectedly impotent and fell limply on the rocks around her. She knew her moment had come and took it. She was not to know that piling up far out at sea was the first of the giant storm waves that had gathered several hundred miles out in the Atlantic, bringing with it all the momentum and violence of the deep ocean.

The rocks were slippery underfoot and more than once Cherry slipped down into seething white rock pools where she had played so often when the tide was out. But she struggled on until, finally, she had climbed high enough to be able to see the thin strip of sand that was all that was left of Boat Cove. It was only a few yards away, so close. Until now she had been crying involuntarily; but now, as she recognised the little path up through the bracken, her heart was lifted with hope and anticipation. She knew that the worst was over, that if the sea would only hold back she would reach the sanctuary of the Cove.

She turned and looked behind her to see how far away the next wave was, just to reassure herself that she had enough time. But the great surge of green water was on her before she could register either disappointment or fear. She was hurled back against the rock below her and covered at once by the sea.

She was conscious as she went down that she was drowning, but she still clutched her shells against her chest and hoped she had enough of them at last to finish the giant's necklace. Those were her last thoughts before the sea took her away.

Cherry lay on her side where the tide had lifted her and coughed until her lungs were clear. She woke as the sea came in once again and frothed around her legs. She rolled on her back, feeling the salt spray on her face and saw that it was night. The sky above her was dashed with stars and the moon rode through the clouds.

She scrambled to her feet, one hand still holding her precious shells close to her. Instinctively she backed away from the sea and looked around her. With growing dismay she saw that she had been thrown back on the wrong side of the rocks, that she was not in Boat Cove. The tide had left only a few feet of sand and rock between her and the cliff face.

There was no way back through the sea to safety.

She turned round to face the cliff that she realised now would be her last hope, for she remembered that this little beach vanished completely at high tide. If she stayed where she was she would surely be swept away again and this time she might not be so fortunate. But the cold seemed to have calmed her and she reasoned more deliberately now, wondering why she had not tried climbing the cliff before. She had hurried into her first attempt at escape and it had very nearly cost her her life. She would wait this time until the sea forced her up the cliff. Perhaps the tide would not come in that far. Perhaps they would be looking for her by now. It was dark. Surely they would be searching. Surely they must find her soon. After all, they knew where she was. Yes, she thought, best just to wait and hope.

She settled down on a ledge of rock that was the first step up on to the cliff face, drew her knees up to her chin to keep out the chill, and waited. She watched as the sea crept ever closer; each wave lashing her with spray and eating away gradually at the beach. She closed her eyes and prayed, hoping against hope that when she opened them the sea would be retreating. But her prayers went unanswered and the sea came in to cover the beach. Once or twice she thought she heard voices above her on the cliff path, but when she called out no one came. She continued to shout for help every few minutes, forgetting it was futile against the continuous roar and hiss of the waves. A pair of raucous white gulls flew down from the cliffs to investigate her and she called to them for help, but they did not seem to understand and wheeled away into the night.

Cherry stayed sitting on her rock until the waves threatened to dislodge her and then reluctantly she began her climb. She would go as far as she needed to and no further. She had scanned the first few feet above for footholds and it did look quite a simple climb to begin with, and so it proved. But her hands were numbed with cold and her legs began to tremble with the strain almost at once. She could see that the ledge she had now reached was the last deep one visible on the cliff face. The shells in her sweater were restricting her freedom of movement so she decided she would leave them there. Wrapped tight in the towel they would be quite safe. She took the soaking bundle out of her sweater and placed it carefully against the rock face on the ledge beside her, pushing it in as far as it would go. 'I'll be back for you,' she said, and reached up for the next lip of rock. Just below her the sea crashed against the cliff as if it wanted to suck her from the rock face and claim her once again. Cherry determined not to look down but to concentrate on the climb.

At first, she imagined that the glow above her was from a torch. She shouted and screamed until she was weak from the effort of it. But although no answering call came from the night, the light remained pale and beckoning, wider than that of a torch. With renewed hope Cherry found enough strength to inch her way up the cliff, until she reached the entrance to a narrow cave. It was filled with a flickering yellow light like that of a candle shaken by the wind. She hauled herself up into the mouth of the cave and sat down exhausted, looking back down at the furious sea frothing beneath her. She laughed aloud in triumph. She was safe! She had defied the sea and won! Her one regret was that she had had to leave her cowrie shells behind. She would fetch them tomorrow after the tide had gone down again.

For the first time now she began to think of her family and how worried they would be, but the thought of walking in through the front door all dripping and dramatic made her almost choke with excitement.

As she reached forward to brush a sharp stone from the sole of her foot, Cherry noticed that the narrow entrance to the cave was half sealed in. She ran her fingers over the stones and cement to make sure, for the light was poor. It was at that moment that she recognised exactly where she was. She recalled now the giant fledgling cuckoo one of her brothers had spotted being fed by a tiny rock pipit earlier in the holidays, how they had quarrelled over the binoculars and how, when she had finally usurped them and made her escape across the rocks, she had found the cuckoo perched at the entrance to a narrow cave some way up the cliff face from the beach.

She had asked about the man-made walling, and her father had told her of the old tin mines whose lodes and adits criss-crossed the entire coastal area around Zennor. This one, he said, might have been the mine they called

Wheel North Grylls, and he thought the adit must have been walled up to prevent the seas from entering the mine in a storm. It was said there had been an accident in the mine only a few years after it was opened over a hundred years before, and that the mine had had to close soon after when the mine owners ran out of money to make the necessary repairs. The entire story came back to her now, and she wondered where the cuckoo was and whether the rock pipit had died with the effort of keeping the fledgling alive. Tin mines, she thought, lead to the surface, and the way home. That thought and her natural inquisitiveness about the source of light persuaded her to her feet and into the tunnel.

The adit became narrower and lower as she crept forward, so that she had to go down on her hands and knees, sometimes flat on her stomach. Although she was out of the wind now, it seemed colder. She felt she was moving downwards for a minute or two, for the blood was coming to her head and her weight was heavy on her hands. Then, quite suddenly, she found the ground levelling out and saw a large tunnel ahead of her. There was no doubt as to which way she should turn, for one way the tunnel was black, and the other way was lighted with candles that lined the lode wall as far as she could see. She called out, 'Anyone there? Anyone there?' She paused to listen for the reply; but all she could hear now was the muffled roar of the sea and the continuous echoing of dripping water.

The tunnel widened now and she found she could walk upright again; but her feet hurt against the stone and so she moved slowly, feeling her way gently with each foot. She had gone only a short distance when she heard the tapping for the first time, distinct and rhythmic, a sound that was instantly recognisable as hammering. It became sharper and noticeably more metallic as she moved up the tunnel. She could hear the distant murmur of voices and the sound of falling stone. Even before she came out of the tunnel and into the vast cave she knew she had happened upon a working mine.

The cave was dark in all but one corner and here she could see two men bending to their work, their backs towards her. One of them was inspecting the rock face closely whilst the other swung his hammer with controlled power, pausing only to spit on his hands from time to time. They wore round hats with turned up brims that served also as candlesticks, for a lighted candle was fixed to each, the light dancing with the shadows along the cave walls as they worked.

Cherry watched for some moments until she made up her mind what to do. She longed to rush up to them and tell of her escape and to ask them to take her to the surface, but a certain shyness overcame her and she held back. Her chance to interrupt came when they sat down against the rock face and opened their canteens. She was in the shadows and they still could not see her.

'Tea looks cold again,' one of them said gruffly. ' 'Tis always cold. I'm sure she makes it wi' cold water.'

'Oh stop your moaning, Father,' said the other, a younger voice, Cherry felt. 'She does her best. She's five little ones to look after and precious little to do it on. She does her best. You mustn't keep on at her so. It upsets her. She does her best.'

'So she does, lad, so she does. And so for that matter do I, but that don't stop her moaning at me and it'll not stop me moaning at her. If we didn't moan at each other, lad, we'd have precious little else to talk about, and that's

18

a fact. She expects of it me, lad, and I expects it of her.'

'Excuse me,' Cherry said tentatively. She felt she had eavesdropped for long enough. She approached them slowly. 'Excuse me, but I've got a bit lost. I climbed the cliff, you see, 'cos I was cut off from the Cove. I was trying to get back, but I couldn't and I saw this light and so I climbed up. I want to get home and I wondered if you could help me get to the top?'

'Top?' said the older one, peering into the dark. 'Come closer, lad, where we can see you.'

'She's not a lad, Father. Are you blind? Can you not see 'tis a filly. 'Tis a young filly, all wet through from the sea. Come,' the young man said, standing up and beckoning Cherry in. 'Don't be afeared, little girl, we shan't harm you. Come on, you can have some of my tea if you like.'

They spoke their words in a manner Cherry had never heard before. It was not the usual Cornish burr, but heavier and rougher in tone, more old-fashioned somehow. There were so many questions in her mind.

'But I thought the mine was closed a hundred years ago,' she said nervously. 'That's what I was told, anyway.'

'Well, you was told wrong,' said the old man, whom Cherry could see more clearly now under his candle. His eyes were white and set far back in his head, unnaturally so, she thought, and his lips and mouth seemed a vivid red in the candlelight.

'Closed, closed indeed, does it look closed to you? D'you think we're digging for worms? Over four thousand tons of tin last year and nine thousand of copper ore, and you ask is the mine closed? Over twenty fathoms below the sea this mine goes. We'll dig right out under the ocean, halfway to 'Merica afore we close down this mine.'

He spoke passionately now, almost angrily, so that Cherry felt she had offended him.

'Hush, Father,' said the young man taking off his jacket and wrapping it round Cherry's shoulders. 'She doesn't want to hear all about that. She's cold and wet. Can't you see? Now let's make a little fire to warm her through. She's shivered right through to her bones. You can see she is.'

'They all are,' said the old tinner pulling himself to his feet. 'They all are.' And he shuffled past her into the dark. 'I'll fetch the wood,' he muttered, and then added, 'for all the good it'll do.'

'What does he mean?' Cherry asked the young man, for whom she felt an instant liking. 'What did he mean by that?'

'Oh pay him no heed, little girl,' he said. 'He's an old man now and tired of the mine. We're both tired of it, but we're proud of it see, and we've nowhere else to go, nothing else to do.'

He had a kind voice that was reassuring to Cherry. He seemed somehow to know the questions she wanted to ask, for he answered them now without her ever asking.

'Sit down by me while you listen, girl,' he said. 'Father will make a fire to warm you and I shall tell you how we come to be here. You won't be afeared now, will you?'

Cherry looked up into his face which was younger than she had expected from his voice; but like his father's, the eyes seemed sad and deep set, yet they smiled at her gently and she smiled back.

'That's my girl. It was a new mine this, promising

everyone said. The best tin in Cornwall and that means the best tin in the world. 1865 it started up and they were looking for tinners, and so Father found a cottage down by Treveal and came to work here. I was already fourteen, so I joined him down the mine. We prospered and the mine prospered, to start with. Mother and the little children had full bellies and there was talk of sinking a fresh shaft. Times were good and promised to be better.'

Cherry sat transfixed as the story of the disaster unfolded. She heard how they had been trapped by a fall of rock, about how they had worked to pull them away, but behind every rock was another rock and another rock. She heard how they had never even heard any sound of rescue. They had died, he said, in two days or so because the air was bad and because there was too little of it.

'Father has never accepted it; he still thinks he's alive, that he goes home to Mother and the little children each evening. But he's dead, just like me. I can't tell him though, for he'd not understand and it would break his heart if he ever knew.'

'So you aren't real. I'm just imaging all this. You're just a dream.'

'No dream, my girl,' said the young man laughing out loud. 'No more'n we're imagining you. We're real right enough, but we're dead and have been for a hundred years and more. Ghosts, spirits, that's what living folk call us. Come to think of it, that's what I called us when I was alive.'

Cherry was on her feet suddenly and backing away.

'No need to be afeared, little girl,' said the young man holding out his hand towards her. 'We won't harm you. No one can harm you, not now. Look, he's started the fire already. Come over and warm yourself. Come, it'll be all right, girl. We'll look after you. We'll help you.'

'But I want to go home,' Cherry said, feeling the panic rising to her voice and trying to control it. 'I know you're kind, but I want to go home. My mother will be worried about me. They'll be out looking for me. Your light saved my life and I want to thank you. But I must go else they'll worry themselves sick, I know they will.'

'You going back home?' the young man asked, and

then he nodded. 'I s'pose you'll want to see your family again.'

'Course I am,' said Cherry perplexed by the question. 'Course I do.'

''Tis a pity,' he said sadly. 'Everyone passes through and no one stays. They all want to go home, but then so do I. You'll want me to guide you to the surface I s'pose.'

'I'm not the first then?' Cherry said. 'There's been others climb up into the mine to escape from the sea? You've saved lots of people.'

'A few,' said the tinner nodding. 'A few.'

'You're a kind person,' Cherry said, warming to the sadness in the young man's voice. 'I never thought ghosts would be kind.'

'We're just people, people who've passed on,' replied the young man, taking her elbow and leading her towards the fire. 'There's nice people and there's nasty people. It's the same if you're alive or if you're dead. You're a nice person, I can tell that, even though I haven't known you for long. I'm sad because I should like to be alive again with my friends and go rabbiting or blackberrying up by the chapel near Treveal like I used to. The sun always seemed to be shining then. After it happened I used to go up to the surface and move amongst the people in the village. I went often to see my family, but if I spoke to them they never seemed to hear me, and of course they can't see you. You can see them, but they can't see you. That's the worst of it. So I don't go up much now, just to collect wood for the fire and a bit of food now and then. I stay down here with Father in the mine and we work away day after day. From time to time someone like you comes up the tunnel from the sea and lightens our darkness. I shall be sad when you go.'

The old man was hunched over the fire rubbing his hands and holding them out over the heat.

'Not often we have a fire,' he said, his voice more spritely now. 'Only on special occasions. Birthdays, of course, we always have a fire on birthdays back at the cottage. Martha's next. You don't know her; she's my only daughter – she'll be eight on September 10th. She's been poorly, you know – her lungs, that's what the doctor said.' He sighed deeply. ''Tis dreadful damp in the cottage. 'Tis well nigh impossible to keep it out.'

There was a tremor in the old man's voice that betrayed his emotion. He looked up at Cherry and she could see the tears in his eyes. 'She looks a bit like you, my dear, raven-haired and as pretty as a picture; but not so tall, not so tall. Come closer, my dear, you'll be warmer that way.'

Cherry sat with them by the fire till it died away to nothing. She longed to go, to get home amongst the living, but the old man talked on of his family and their little one-roomed cottage with a ladder to the bedroom where they all huddled together for warmth, of his friends that used to meet in the Tinners' Arms every evening. There were tales of wrecking and smuggling, and all the while the young man sat silent, until there was a lull in the story.

'Father,' he said. 'I think our little friend would like to go home now. Shall I take her up as I usually do?' The old man nodded and waved his hand in dismissal.

'Come back and see us sometime, if you've a mind to,' he said, and then put his face in his hands.

'Goodbye,' said Cherry. 'Thank you for the fire and

for helping me. I won't forget you.' But the old man never replied.

The journey through the mine was long and difficult. She held fast to the young tinner's waist as they walked silently through the dark tunnels, stopping every now and then to climb a ladder to the lode above until finally they could look up the shaft above them and see the daylight.

'It's dawn,' said the young man, looking up.

'I'll be back in time for breakfast,' said Cherry setting her foot on the ladder.

'You'll remember me?' the young tinner asked, and Cherry nodded, unable to speak through her tears. She felt a strange affinity with him and his father. 'And if you should ever need me, come back again. You may need me and I shall be here. I go nowhere else.'

'Thank you,' said Cherry. 'I won't forget. I doubt anyone is going to believe me when I tell them about you. No one believes in ghosts, not up there.'

'I doubt it too. Be happy, little friend,' he said. And he was gone, back into the tunnel. Cherry waited until the light from the candle in his hat had vanished and then turned eagerly to the ladder and began to climb up towards the light.

She found herself in a place she knew well, high on the moor by Zennor Quoit. She stood by the ruined mine workings and looked down at the sleeping village shrouded in mist, and the calm blue sea beyond. The storm had passed and there was scarcely a breath of wind even on the moor. It was only ten minutes' walk down through the bracken, across the road by the Eagle's Nest and down the farm track to the cottage where her family would be waiting. She began to run, but the clothes were still heavy and wet and she was soon reduced to a fast walk. All the while she was determining where she would begin her story, wondering how much they would believe. At the top of the lane she stopped to consider how best to make her entrance. Should she ring the bell and be found standing there, or should she just walk in and surprise them there at breakfast? She longed to see the joy on their faces, to feel the warmth of their arms round her and to bask once again in their affection.

She saw as she came round the corner by the cottage

that there was a long blue Land Rover parked in the lane, bristling with aerials. '*Coastguard*' she read on the side. As she came down the steps she noticed that the back door of the cottage was open and she could hear voices inside. She stole in on tiptoe. The kitchen was full of uniformed men drinking tea, and around the table sat her family, dejection and despair etched on every face. They hadn't seen her yet. One of the uniformed men had put down his cup and was speaking. His voice was low and hushed.

'You're sure the towel is hers, no doubts about it?'

Cherry's mother shook her head.

'It's her towel,' she said quietly, 'and they are her shells. She must have put them up there, must have been the last thing she did.'

Cherry saw her shells spread out on the open towel and stifled a shout of joy.

'We have to say,' he went on. 'We have to say then, most regrettably, that the chances of finding your daughter alive now are very slim. It seems she must have tried to climb the cliff to escape the heavy seas and fallen in. We've scoured the cliff top for miles in both directions and covered the entire beach, and there's no sign of her. She must have been washed out to sea. We must conclude that she is missing. We have to presume that she is drowned.'

Cherry could listen no longer but burst into the room shouting.

'I'm home, I'm home. Look at me, I'm not drowned at all. I'm here! I'm home!'

The tears were running down her face.

But no one in the room even turned to look in her direction. Her brothers cried openly, one of them clutching the giant's necklace.

'But it's me,' she shouted again. 'Me, can't you see? It's me and I've come back. I'm all right. Look at me.'

But no one did, and no one heard.

The giant's necklace lay spread out on the table.

'So she'll never finish it after all,' said her mother softly. 'Poor Cherry. Poor dear Cherry.'

And in that one moment Cherry knew and understood that she was right, that she would never finish her necklace, that she belonged no longer with the living but had passed on beyond.

THE WHITE HORSE OF ZENNOR

THE FAMILY HAD FARMED THE LAND IN THE
Foage Valley at Zennor for over five hundred years. They
had been there it was said ever since Miguel Veluna first
crawled ashore half-drowned at Porthzennor Cove from
the wreck of his galleon off Gunnards Head. As soon as
he could make himself understood, so the story goes, he
married the farmer's daughter who had just nursed him
back to life; and with her came the farm in the fertile
valley that runs down from the north coast to the south
with the high moors rising on either side. Through the

generations the Velunas prospered, sowing their corn along the sheltered fields and grazing their hardy cattle on the moors above. They became tough and circumspect, as are all the farmers whose roots lie deep in the rocks and soil of Penwith, the last bastion of land against the mighty Atlantic that seeks with every storm to subdue the peninsula and to rejoin the Channel a few short miles to the south. Over the centuries the family had survived famine and disease, invasion and depression; but now the Velunas were staring ruin in the face and there seemed no way forward for them.

Farmer Veluna had been a joyful soul all his life, a man of laughter, who rode high through the fields on his tractor, forever singing his heart out, in a perpetual celebration that he belonged where he was. His joy in life was infectious so that he spread around him a convivial sense of security and happiness. In business he was always fair although he was thought to be over-generous at times, not hard enough a man according to some of the more craggy moorland farmers. But no one in the parish was better respected and liked than Farmer Veluna so that when he married lovely Molly Parson from Morvah and produced a daughter and a son within two years, everyone thought it was no more than he deserved. When he built a new milking parlour some of his friends shook their heads and wondered, for no one could recall a milking herd on the land before; but they knew Farmer Veluna to be level-headed and hardworking. No one doubted that if anyone could make it work he could, and certainly everyone wished him well in his new venture.

For several years the milk flowed and the profits came. He built up the finest herd of Guernsey cows for miles around and there was talk that he was doing so well that he might take on more land. Then, within six short weeks he was a ruined man. First the corn harvest failed completely, a summer storm lashing through the valley breaking the ripened corn and flattening it to the ground. The storm was followed by weeks of heavy drizzle so that not even the straw could be salvaged. But the cows were still milking and the regular milk cheque was always there every month to see them through. Farmer Veluna was disappointed by the setback but burned off the straw when he could and began to plough again. He was still singing on his tractor.

Then came the annual Ministry check for brucellosis,* the outcome of which had never worried Farmer Veluna. It was routine, no more than that, so that when the two vets arrived at his front door some days later it never even occurred to him that they had come about the brucellosis test. The vets knew him well and liked him for he was good to his stock and paid his bills, so they broke the news to him as gently as they could. Farmer Veluna stood in the doorway, his heart heavy with foreboding as they began to tell him the worst.

'There can be no mistake?' he said. 'You're sure there's no mistake?' But he knew he need not have asked.

'It's brucellosis, Farmer, no doubt about it; right through the herd. I'm sorry, but you know what has to be done,' said one of the vets, putting a hand on his shoulder to comfort him. 'It has to be done today. The Ministry men are on their way. We've come to help.'

* a highly contagious disease that kills calves before they are born.

Farmer Veluna nodded slowly and they went inside together.

That afternoon his entire herd of golden Guernseys was driven into the yard below the dairy and killed. Every cow and calf on the farm, even one born that same morning, was slaughtered; and the milking parlour stood silent from that day on.

In the weeks that followed the disaster every tractor and saleable machine had to be sold for there was the family to feed as well as the other stock, and an overdraft at the bank that Farmer Veluna had to honour. It was not much money to find each month but with little coming in, it soon became apparent that the pigs had to be sold, then the geese and finally the beloved horse. All that was left were a few hens and a shed full of redundant rusting machinery.

Each evening the family would sit around the kitchen table and talk over the possibilities, but as the situation worsened the children noticed that it was their mother who emerged the stronger. The light had gone out of their father's eye, his entire demeanour was clouded over with despair. Even his jaunty, lurruping walk had slowed, and he moved aimlessly around the farm now as if in a daze. He seemed scarcely even willing or able to consider any suggestions for the future. His wife, Molly, managed to persuade him to go to the bank to ask for an extension of the loan, and for a new loan to finance new stock and seed; but times were hard even for the banks and when both were refused he lapsed into a profound depression that pervaded every room in the house.

Friends and neighbours came with offers of help but he thanked them kindly for their generosity and refused them politely as they knew he would, for he was above all a proud man from a proud family and not accustomed to accepting charity from anyone, however dire the necessity.

Desperately Molly urged him on, trying to release him from the prison of his despair, believing in her heart that he had it in him to recover and knowing that without him they were lost. The two children meanwhile sought their own consolation and relief up on the high moors they knew and loved so well. They would leave the house and farm behind them, and climb up to the great granite cheesewring rocks above the village where the wind blew in so fiercely from the sea that they could lean into it with arms outstretched and be held and buffeted like kites. They would leap from rock to rock like mountain goats, play endless hide-and-seek and tramp together over the boggy moors, all the while trying to forget the threat that hung over them. Their walks would end often on the same logan stone above the Eagle's Nest, a giant slab of rounded granite as finely balanced as a pair of scales on the rock below, so that if they stood on opposite ends they could rock it up and down like a seesaw.

Here they were sitting one early autumn evening with the sun setting fire to the sea beyond Zennor when they saw their father and mother climbing up through the bracken towards them. Unusually, they were holding hands and that signified to both children that a decision might have been reached. They instinctively sensed what the decision was and dreaded it. Annie decided she would forestall them.

'You needn't tell us,' Annie said to them as they climbed up to sit down beside the children on the logan stone. 'We know already. There's no other way is there?'

'What do you know, Annie?' said Farmer Veluna, the first words either of the children had heard him utter for more than a week.

'That we're going to sell the farm,' she said softly, almost as if she did not wish to hear it. 'We're going to sell the farm and move away, aren't we?'

'I won't go,' said Arthur, shrugging off his mother's arm. 'I won't. I was born here and I'm going to stay here. No one is going to make me move.'

He spoke with grim resolve.

At nine, he was a year younger than his sister but at that moment he seemed suddenly a great deal older. He was already as tall as Annie, and even as an infant others had recognised in him that strong Veluna spirit.

'We shall have to sell, Arthur,' said his father. 'We've no alternative. You need money to run a farm and we haven't got any. It's that simple. Everything we had was in the cows and now they're gone. I'm not going to argue about it; there's no point. We shall have to sell up and buy a smaller farm elsewhere. That's all there is to it. There's other farms and there's other places.'

'Not like this one,' Arthur said and turned to his father, tears filling his eyes. 'There's no place like this place and you know it. So don't pretend. You told me often enough, father; you told me never to give up and now you're giving up yourself.' Farmer Veluna looked away unable to give his son any answer that would convince even himself.

'That's unkind, Arthur,' said his mother. 'You mustn't be unkind to your father, not now. He's done all he can - you know he has. It'll be all right. It'll be the same. We shall go on farming, but in a smaller way, that's all. It's all your father can do; you must see that Arthur.'

Annie turned to her father and put her arms around him as much to comfort herself as to comfort him. It seemed to do neither.

Farmer stroked his daughter's hair gently.

'We shall be all right, Annie,' he said. 'I promise you that. Don't worry, I'm not a man to break my promises. You know that, don't you?'

Annie nodded into his chest, fighting back her tears.

'We'll see you back at home, children,' Molly said.

'Don't be long now. It gets cold up here when the sun's gone.'

The two children sat side by side and watched their parents move slowly back down the hill towards the farm. They were so alike to look at that many people considered them to be twins. Both had their parents' dark shining hair and their skin stayed dark even in the winter. They had few friends besides each other for there were not many children of their own age on other farms round about, and so they had spent much of their life together, and by now sensed each other's mood intuitively.

'Annie,' Arthur said finally when he had wiped the tears away from his cheeks. 'I couldn't live anywhere else, could you? We have to find a way to stay here, because I'm not going. I don't care what father says, I'm not going.'

But Annie was not listening to her brother, for she had been distracted some moments before by the sound of a distant voice from behind her, perhaps from the direction of the Quoit. She had thought it might be the wind at first, moaning through the stones. She put her hand on her brother's arm.

'Listen,' she said. And the voice was still there, clearly discernible now that Arthur had stopped talking. It was more distinct now, and although they could as yet make out no words, they could tell that someone was calling out for help. They leapt from the logan stone and ran down the track into the heather and bracken of the high moor, homing in all the while on the plaintive cry that came to them ever more urgently from across the moor. They could hear now that it came from the ruins of the old count-house, and they slowed to a walk as they approached, suddenly uncertain of themselves.

'Help me, please help me,' clearly a man's voice, a man in pain; and no longer a shout into the wilderness, but a plea directed to them.

'Can you see anyone?' Annie said, clutching Arthur's arm in fright.

'I'm down here, over here in the ruins. Oh for pity's sake, come quickly.' The children climbed slowly down into the ruin itself, Annie still holding on to her brother, and at last they found what they had been looking for.

Lying in the corner of the ruined old count-house, propped up against a granite pillar was an old man, but no ordinary man; for he was smaller even than any dwarf but unlike a dwarf his features were in perfect proportion to his size. He was roughly clothed in heavy tweed trousers and a black moleskin jacket. He had wild white hair and eyes as blue as the sea. He lay with one knee clasped to his chest and the children saw that clinging grotesquely to his foot was a rusty gin trap.

'A Knocker,' Annie whispered, and she stepped back in alarm, dragging Arthur back with her; but Arthur wrenched himself free and stood his ground.

'I know that,' Arthur said, speaking loudly for he felt it was rude to whisper. 'There's nothing wrong with Knockers. They won't hurt you, 'less you hurt them. Isn't that right, sir?'

'Quite right, young fellow,' said the old man crisply, 'and anyway since I'm pinioned here with this confounded trap, there's not too much danger of my hurting you my girl, now is there?'

Annie shook her head vigorously but was not convinced.

'And since you're here I wonder, would it be too much trouble to ask you to help me out of this thing? I would have done it myself if I could, but I'm a wee bit little to pull the spring back and if I move, my leg burns like hell fire. Confounded farmers,' he went on, wincing in pain, 'they're still trapping you know, but it's not as bad as it was. In the old days my father told me the whole moor was littered with them – rabbit traps, bird traps, fox traps, all sorts. You couldn't go out at dark you know for fear of putting your foot in it, so to speak. This is an old one, been here for years I should think, but there's still some of them at it. I've seem them. I know everything that goes on. Confounded farmers.'

'I'm a farmer's son,' said Arthur defensively, crouching down to examine the trap, 'and my father wouldn't use gin traps. He says they're cruel and anyway they're not allowed any more.'

'Quite right,' the Knocker said, straightening out his leg for Arthur. 'I know your father. He's a good man. Know you two as well – seen you often enough springing around out on those rocks. Didn't know I was watching, did you? 'Course it's a shame about your farm, but that's life. Swings and roundabouts, ups and downs. It happens.'

'You've watched us?' said Annie who had plucked up enough courage at last to come closer. 'You've seen us up there?'

'Course I have,' said the Knocker. 'We know everyone for miles around. It's our job to know what's going on; that's what we're here for. Now look, children, can we continue this discussion after you've set me free, if you don't mind. My leg's throbbing and I'll bleed to death if you don't help me out of this soon.'

Rust had stiffened the spring so it took Arthur and Annie some time to prise open the jaws of the trap far enough for the Knocker to withdraw his boot. He fell back to the ground in a faint as the boot came clear. By the time he came to, some minutes later, he found the children had taken his boot off and were kneeling over him bathing his ankle with a wet handkerchief. He lifted himself onto his elbows and smiled up at them.

'That was kind of you,' he said. 'I'm surprised you didn't run away; most people would have you know. I think you must know about us. Someone must've told you. But you didn't know we bled, did you?'

Arthur shook his head. 'No, but everyone's heard about you,' he said, 'although no one really believes in you any more. But ever since my mother told us all about Knockers and little people and all that, I've always thought that if you were true then you'd live up here on the moor or maybe down the mines. There's nowhere else for you, is there?'

'I still don't think I should really believe it,' said Annie, tying the handkerchief in a tight knot, 'if I wasn't touching you, I'm sure I wouldn't.'

'The leg will be fine now, right as rain, good as new,' said the Knocker.

His pale face was deeply lined with age and there was a kindness and a wisdom in his face that both the children trusted instinctively.

'Thank you,' he said as the children helped him to his feet.

He shook them each solemnly by the hand.

'Thank you both very kindly. I don't think I should have survived a frosty autumn night out here on the moor. I'm old you see and even Knockers die when they get old you know. It's so nice to find people who'll talk to us. So many people just run away and it's such a pity, because there's nothing to be frightened of.'

He hobbled unaided around the ruined count-house testing his leg before returning to the children.

'No broken bones I think. All's well that ends well, as they say.'

'Will you be all right now?' Arthur asked. 'We ought to be getting back home now. Father said we should be off the moor by dark.'

'Quite right. Wise man, your father,' the little Knocker said, brushing off his moleskin jacket and pulling it down straight. 'After all, you never know who you might bump into up here. The place is full of spriggans and pixies and nasty wee little folk and even,' he whispered low, 'even the odd Knocker or two.' And the three laughed together as old friends might do over a confidential joke. 'But before you go, children, I have to thank you properly. One good turn deserves another, tit for tat, you scratch my back, I'll scratch yours, and so on. I want each of you to close your eyes and tell me your one dearest wish. You have to say what you'd most like in all the world. Ask and you shall have it. Annie, you're first. Come on now.'

Annie did not have to think for long.

'A horse,' she said, her eyes squeezed tight shut. 'We had to sell our horse you see, because father needed the money for the farm. I've always wanted a great white horse.'

'Keep your eyes closed,' said the Knocker. 'Keep them closed both of you and don't open them until I tell you. Now you Arthur. What is it that you'd most want in all the world?'

'I want to stay here on the farm,' said Arthur slowly. 'I want my father to be happy again and to go singing on his tractor. I want the animals back and the farm working again like it used to.'

'That's a lot of wants,' said the Knocker. 'Let's see what we can do now.'

He chuckled aloud, and his voice seemed more animated now.

'You know, children, I haven't had the chance to do this for donkey's years. I'm so excited, I feel like a little Knocker all over again. You wished for the horse, Annie; and you wished for the farm back as it was, Arthur. How you do it is up to you, but you'll find enough seed corn in the barn when you get back home and you can use the horse as you wish. But after a year and a day you must bring the horse back here to me and leave twelve sacks of good seed corn back in your barn to repay me. Do you understand? Remember, be back here by dusk a year and a day from now.'

'We'll be here,' said Arthur.

'Promise?' said the Knocker.

'We promise,' they said solemnly.

'You should be able to manage everything by that time with luck, and I'll see you have enough of that. All right children, open your eyes now.'

In place of the little Knocker stood a giant of a horse, towering above them, a brilliant white from mane to tail. He looked down at the children almost causally, swished his tail, shook his head with impatience and then sprang out over the ruined wall and onto the open moor beyond where he stood waiting in the bracken for the scrambling children to catch him up.

Arthur had never been fond of horses. They seemed to him to be unpredictable creatures and he had always steered clear of them. Anyway, as a budding farmer he had no use for any animal that was not productive. But Annie had enough confidence and experience for both of them and she caught him gently by the mane and stroked his nose, speaking softly to him all the while. Within a few minutes they were both mounted on the great white horse and were trotting down the hillside and into the farmyard where the chickens scattered in panic at their approach. The noise brought Farmer Veluna and Molly running out of the back door where they were faced with the terrifying spectacle of their two children perched precariously up on a massive white stallion of at least seventeen hands, that snorted in excitement, tossing its head and pawing the yard, sending sparks flying along the cobbles into the dark.

Arthur told their story breathlessly. With the evidence of the horse before their eyes and the obvious sincerity in Arthur's voice, it was difficult for his father or mother to harbour any doubt but that the story was indeed true. Certainly they knew Arthur had a wild and fertile imagination and was impetuous enough at times but with Annie sitting astride the horse in front of him, laughing aloud with delight and adding her own details from time to time, both Farmer and Molly were very soon completely convinced.

'Look in the barn, Father,' Arthur proclaimed with absolute confidence. 'The little man said there'd be enough seed corn in there to make a start. We can save the farm, Father, I know we can. The seed will be there, I'm sure of it. Have a look, Father.'

Farmer Veluna crossed the yard on his own and opened wide the great barn doors. They saw the light go on, bathing the yard in a yellow glow, and they heard a whoop of joy before Farmer Veluna came running out again. He was laughing as he used to laugh.

'Well I'll eat my hat,' he said, and stuffed the peak of his flat cap into his mouth. Annie and Arthur knew then they had found their father again. 'We have a horse and we have the seed,' Farmer Veluna said. 'There's all my father's old horsedrawn equipment in the old cart shed, and I think I know where I can find his old set of harness. It's up in the attic, isn't it Molly?' But he did not wait for a reply. 'It may be a bit small for this giant of a horse, but it'll stretch. It'll fit – it's got to fit. 'Course,

I've never worked a horse, but father did and I watched him years ago and followed him often enough in the fields. I'll pick it up; it shouldn't be too difficult. We've a chance,' he said. 'We've a chance, children, a sporting chance.'

And from that moment on there was no more talk of selling up.

Ploughing started the following morning just after dawn. The ground was just dry enough, the earth turning cleanly from the shares. The horse proved tireless in the fields. They had sold every bale of hay so he had to pick enough sustenance from the cold wet autumn grass; but that seemed to be enough for him, for the horse ploughed on that day well into the evening, and came back for more the next day and the next and the next.

It was clear at the outset that the horse had an uncanny instinct for the land. He knew how tight to turn, what speed to go without ever having to be told. When his father tired, Arthur could walk behind the plough and simply follow the horse down the furrows and around the headlands until the job was done. If he stumbled and fell in the furrows, as he often did, the horse would wait for him to regain his feet before leaning again into his harness, taking the strain and plodding off down the field.

Within three weeks all the corn fields along the valley were ploughed, harrowed and drilled with barley. Word spread quickly around the parish that Farmer Veluna was laughing again and they came visiting once more to stand at the gate with him and admire his miraculous workhorse.

'No diesel, nothing to go wrong; he'll plough the steepest land on the farm,' Farmer would say with expansive pride. 'Built like a tank but gentle as a lamb. See for yourself. Arthur can manage him on his own and he's only nine you know. Have you ever seen anything like it?'

'Where the devil did you get him from?' they would ask because they had heard all kinds of rumours.

And he would tell them the story of the little Knocker man on the moor who had come to their rescue, but no one believed him. The farmers amongst them laughed knowingly at the story and told Farmer

Veluna to pull the other one; but they did not press him for they knew well enough that a farmer will never disclose the source of his good fortune. But at home their wives knew better and the story of the amazing white horse of Zennor spread along the coast like thistledown in the wind. But in spite of their scepticism all their friends were delighted to see Farmer Veluna his old self again, and they determined to help him succeed. So one winter's night in the Tinners' Arms they got together and worked out how they might help the Farmer back on his feet whether he wanted their help or not. They knew he was proud, as they were, so that any help had to be both anonymous and unreturnable.

So it was that on Christmas morning when Farmer Veluna and his family returned home after church, they found their yard filled with milling animals, three sows and a boar, half a dozen geese, five cows with suckling calves and at least twenty-five ewes. Puzzled and not a little suspicious, Farmer Veluna phoned all around the parish to find out who owned the wandering animals that had converged on his yard, but no one seemed to know anything about them and no one claimed them.

He was about to contact the police in Penzance when Arthur and Annie came running into the kitchen, their voices shrill with excitement.

'The barn,' Annie shouted. 'It's full, full of hay and straw.'

'And there's feed,' Arthur said. 'Sacks and sacks of it, enough to last us through the winter.'

'It's that Knocker again,' Farmer Veluna said, and the children believed him; but Molly, with a woman's intuition, knew better but said nothing.

The winter was long and hard that year, but with the sounds of the farm all around them again and the winter corn shooting up green in the fields, Farmer and his family were more than content. The white horse wintered out in a sheltered field behind the old granary. He grew a long white shaggy coat so that he seemed even more vast than ever. Whenever he was not needed hauling the dung cart or carrying hay bales out to the cattle on the farm, Annie would ride him out over the moor and down through the fields to the cliffs. He was of course far too big for her to control, but she had no fear of horses and found that no control was needed anyway. A gentle word in his ear, a pat of encouragement on his great arching neck and he would instantly do what she wanted. It was not obedience and Annie recognised that; it was simply that the horse wished to please her. He would go like the wind, jump any ditch or fence he was asked to and seemed as sure-footed on the hills as a goat. But it was on one of these rides that Annie first discovered that he had an inclination to make his way towards the cliffs, and once there he would stand looking out to the open sea, ears pricked to the cry of the wheeling gulls and the thunder of the surf against the cliffs. He was always reluctant to turn away for home, calling out at the last over his shoulder and turning back his ears as if expecting some kind of reply.

After just such a ride Annie finally decided upon a name for the horse. No name seemed to have suited until now. 'He'll be called Pegasus,' she declared, and no-one argued for she had become vehemently possessive, scolding both Arthur and her father if they worked him too hard on the farm or did not look after him as well as she thought they should have done. She groomed him regularly every morning and picked out his feet. She it was who towelled him down after work and rubbed in the soothing salted water so that the harness would not make him sore. She was passionately proud of him and would ride tall through the village when she rode out with the hunt, soaking in the admiration and envy of both riders and spectators alike. There was not a horse in the parish to touch him and even other horses seemed to sense it, moving nervously away whenever he approached. There were some who doubted that any horse could jump just as well as he could plough, but when they witnessed his performance in the chase any doubts vanished at once. Where others pulled aside to find a lower hedge or a narrower ditch, Pegasus sailed over with apparent ease. He out-paced every horse in the field and Annie used no whip and no spur, for none were needed. He was, she said glowingly when she got back home, as strong as any tractor, as bold as a hunter, and as fast as a racehorse. Pegasus had become a local celebrity and Annie basked in his reflected glory.

With the spring drying out the land Pegasus turned carthorse once more and was hitched up for the spring ploughing. Farmer Veluna had enough seed for two small fields of oats and Pegasus went to it with a will; but both Arthur and his father now noticed that the horse would pause, ears pricked, at the end of the furrow nearest to the sea; and it was quite apparent that the furrows going down the hill towards the cliffs in the distance were sometimes ploughed more quickly and therefore less deeply than the furrows leading back to the farmhouse.

'Most horses speed up on the way back home; that's what I thought,' said Farmer Veluna. 'Can't understand it, doesn't make sense.'

'But you can't expect him to behave like an ordinary horse, father,' said Arthur, ''cos he isn't an ordinary horse. Just look at him father, he'd plough this field all on his own if you let him. Go on Father, try it, let him do it.'

Farmer Veluna let go of the plough more to please his son than anything else and allowed the horse to move on alone. As they watched in amazement the plough remained straight as an arrow, and inch perfect in depth. Pegasus turned slowly and came back towards them, his line immaculate and parallel. Arthur and his father picked the stones out of the furrows as evening fell while Pegasus ploughed up and down the field until the last furrow was complete. Then they ran over the field towards him to guide him round the headlands, but Pegasus had already turned and was making the first circuit of the field. At that moment both Arthur and his father finally understood what Annie already knew, that this was a miraculous creature that needed no help from them or from anyone.

Annie fitted in her rides whenever she thought Pegasus was rested enough after his work, but as the blackthorn withered and the fuchsia began to bud in the early summer, Pegasus was more and more occupied on the farm. At the end of June he cut a fine crop of sweet meadow hay, turned it and baled it. He took cartloads of farmyard manure out into the fields for spreading. He cut thistles and docks and bracken in the steeper fields up near the moor. Hitched up with a great chain he pulled huge granite rocks out of the ground and dragged them into the hedgerows. In the blazing heat of high summer he hauled the water tanks out onto the furthest fields and in August harvested the corn he had drilled the autumn before.

The barley crop was so rich that summer that Farmer Veluna was able to sell so much to the merchants that he could buy in more suckling cows and calves, as well as his first ten milking cows, the beginnings of his new dairy herd. As autumn began the milking parlour throbbed into life once more, but he had not forgotten to keep back twelve sacks of seed corn that he owed to the little Knocker.

The sows had farrowed well and there were already fat pigs to sell; and some of the lambs were already big enough to go to market. The hens were laying well, even in the heat and the goslings would be ready for Christmas.

But in spite of the recovery and all it meant to the family, the mood of the farmhouse was far from happy, for as the summer nights shortened and the blackberries ripened in the hedgerows, they knew that their year with Pegasus was almost over. Annie spent all her time now with him, taking him out every day for long rides down to the cliffs where she knew he loved to be. Until dusk each evening she would sit astride him, gazing with him out to sea, before turning him away and walking slowly up Trevail Valley, through Wicca Farm and back home over the moor.

When the time came that September evening, a year and a day from the first meeting with the Knocker, Annie and Arthur led the horse by his long white mane up onto the high moors. Arthur wanted to comfort his sister for he could feel the grief she was suffering. He said nothing but put his hand into hers and clasped it tight. As they neared the cheesewring rocks and moved out along the track across the moor towards the ruined count house, Pegasus lifted his head and whinnied excitedly. There was a new spring in his step and his ears twitched back and forth as they approached the count-house. Annie let go of his mane and whispered softly. 'Off you go, Pegasus,' she said. Pegasus looked down at her as if reassuring himself that she meant what she said, and then trotted out ahead of them and down into the ruins until he was hidden from their view. The children followed him, clambering laboriously over the walls.

As they dropped down into the count house they saw that the horse was gone and in his place was the little old Knocker, who waved to them cheerily. 'Good as your word,' he said.

'So were you,' Arthur said. 'Father is a happy man again and it won't be long before we'll be milking fifty cows like we were before. Father says we'll be able to afford a tractor soon.'

'Where's he gone?' Annie asked in a voice as composed as her tears would allow. 'Where's Pegasus gone?'

'Out there,' said the Knocker pointing out to sea. 'Look out there. Can you see the white horses playing, d'you see their waving manes? Can you hear them calling? Don't be sad, Annie,' he said kindly. 'He loves it out there with his friends. A year on the land was a year of exile for him. But you were so good to him, Annie, and for that reason he'll come back to you this one night in every year. That's a promise. Be here up on the moor and he'll come every year for as long as you want him to.'

And he does come, one autumn night in every year as the old Knocker promised. So if you happen to be walking up towards Zennor Quoit one moon-bright autumn night with the mists hovering over the valley and the sea shining below the Eagle's Nest, and if you hear the pounding of hoof beats and see a white horse come out of the moon and thunder over the moor, you will know that it is Annie, Annie and the white horse of Zennor.

'GONE TO SEA'

WILLIAM TREGERTHEN HAD THE LOOK OF A child who carried all the pain of the world on his hunched shoulders. But he had not always been like this. He is remembered by his mother as the happy, chortling child of his infancy, content to bask in his mother's warmth and secure in the knowledge that the world was made just for him. But with the ability to walk came the slow understanding that he walked differently from others and that this was to set him apart from everyone he loved. He found he could not run with his brothers through the high hay fields, chasing after rabbits; that he could not clamber with them down the rocks to the sea but had to wait at the top of the cliffs and watch them hop-scotching over the boulders and leaping in and out of the rock pools below.

He was the youngest of four brothers born onto a farm that hung precariously along the rugged cliffs below the Eagle's Nest. The few small square fields that made up the farm were spread, like a green patchwork between the granite farmhouse and the grey-grim sea, merging into gorse and bracken as they neared the cliff top. For a whole child it was a paradise of adventure and mystery, for the land was riddled with deserted tin miners' cottages and empty, ivy-clad chapels that had once been filled with boisterous hymns and sonorous prayer. There were deserted wheel houses that loomed out of the mist, and dark, dank caves that must surely have been used by wreckers and smugglers. Perhaps they still were.

But William was not a whole child; his left foot was turned inwards and twisted. He shuffled along behind his older brothers in a desperate attempt to stay with them and to be part of their world. His brothers were not hard-souled children, but were merely wrapped in their own fantasies. They were pirates and smugglers and revenue men, and the shadowing presence of William was beginning already to encroach on their freedom of movement. As he grew older he was left further and further behind and they began to ignore him, and then to treat him as if he were not there. Finally, when William was just about school age, they rejected him outright for the first time. 'Go home to Mother,' they said. 'She'll look after you.'

William did not cry, for by now it came as no shock to him. He had already been accustomed to the aside remarks, the accusing fingers in the village and the assiduously averted eyes. Even his own father, with whom he had romped and gambolled as an infant, was becoming estranged and would leave him behind more and more when he went out on the farm. There were fewer rides on the tractor these days, fewer invitations to ride up in front of him on his great shining horse. William knew that he had become a nuisance. What he could not know was that an inevitable guilt had soured his father who found he could no longer even look on his son's stumbling gait without a shudder of shame. He was not a cruel man by nature, but he did not want to have to be reminded continually of his own inadequacy as a father and as a man.

Only his mother stood by him and William loved her for it. With her he could forget his hideous foot that would never straighten and that caused him to lurch whenever he moved. They talked of the countries over the sea's end, beyond where the sky fell like a curtain on the horizon. From her he learned about the wild birds and the flowers. Together they would lie hidden in the bracken watching the foxes at play and counting the seals as they bobbed up and down at sea. It was rare enough for his mother to leave her kitchen but whenever she could she would take William out through the fields and clamber up onto a granite rock that rose from the soil below like an iceberg. From here they could look up to Zennor Quoit above them and across the fields towards the sea. Here she would tell him all the stories of Zennor. Sitting beside her, his knees drawn up under his chin, he would bury himself in the mysteries of this wild place. He heard of mermaids, of witches, of legends as old as the rock itself and just as enduring. The bond between mother and son grew strong during these years; she would be there by his side wherever he went. She became the sole prop of William's life, his last link with happiness; and for his mother her last little son kept her soul singing in the midst of an endless drudgery.

For William Tregerthen, school was a nightmare of misery. Within his first week he was dubbed 'Limping Billy'. His brothers, who might have afforded some protection, avoided him and left him to the mercy of the mob. William did not hate his tormentors any more than he hated wasps in September; he just wished they would go away. But they did not. 'Limping Billy' was a source of infinite amusement that few could resist. Even the children William felt might have been friends to him were seduced into collaboration. Whenever they were tired of football or of tag or skipping, there was always 'Limping Billy' sitting by himself on the playground wall under the fuchsia hedge. William would see them coming and screw up his courage, turning on his thin smile of resignation that he hoped might soften their hearts. He continued to smile through the taunting and the teasing, through the limping competitions that they forced him to judge. He would nod appreciatively at their attempts to mimic the Hunchback of Notre Dame, and conceal his dread and his humiliation when they invited him to do better. He trained himself to laugh with them back at himself; it was his way of riding the punches.

His teachers were worse, cloaking their revulsion under a veneer of pity. To begin with they over-burdened him with a false sweetness and paid him far too much loving attention; and then because he found the words difficult to spell and his handwriting was uneven and awkward, they began to assume, as many do, that one unnatural limb somehow infects the whole and turns a cripple into an idiot. Very soon he was dismissed by his teachers as unteachable and ignored thereafter.

It did not help either that William was singularly un-childlike in his appearance. He had none of the cherubic innocence of a child; there was no charm about him, no redeeming feature. He was small for his age; but his face carried already the mark of years. His eyes were dark and deep-set, his features pinched and sallow. He walked with a stoop, dragging his foot behind him like a leaden weight. The world had taken him and shrivelled him up already. He looked permanently gaunt and hungry as he sat staring out of the classroom window at the heaving sea beyond the fields. A recluse was being born.

On his way back from school that last summer, William tried to avoid the road as much as possible. Meetings always became confrontations, and there was never anyone who wanted to walk home with him. He himself wanted less and less to be with people. Once into the fields and out of sight of the road he would break into a staggering, ugly run, swinging out his twisted foot, straining to throw it forward as far as it would go. He would time himself across the field that ran down from the road to the hay barn, and then throw himself at last face down and exhausted into the sweet warmth of new hay. He had done this for a few days already and, according to his counting, his time was improving with each run. But as he lay there now panting in the hay he heard someone clapping high up in the haystack behind him. He sat up quickly and looked around. It was a face he knew, as familiar to him as the rocks in the fields around the farm, an old face full of deeply etched crevasses and raised veins, unshaven and red with drink. Everyone around the village knew Sam, or 'Sam the Soak' as he was called, but no-one knew much about him. He lived alone in a cottage in the churchtown up behind the Tinners' Arms, cycling every day into St. Ives where he kept a small fishing boat and a few lobster pots. He was a fair-weather fisherman, with a ramshackle boat that only went to sea when the weather was set fair. Whenever there were no fish or no lobsters to be found, or when the weather was blowing up, he would stay on shore and drink. It was rumoured there had been some great tragedy in his life before he came to live at Zennor, but he never spoke of it so no-one knew for certain.

'A fine run, Billy,' said Sam; his drooping eyes smiled gently. There was no sarcasm in his voice but rather a kind sincerity that William warmed to instantly.

'Better'n yesterday anyway,' William said.

'You should swim, dear lad,' Sam sat up and shook the hay out of his hair. He clambered down the haystack towards William, talking as he came. 'If I had a foot like that, dear lad, I'd swim. You'd be fine in the water, swim like the seals I shouldn't wonder.' He smiled awkwardly and ruffled William's hair. 'Got a lot to do. Hope you didn't mind my sleeping awhile in your hay. Your father makes good hay, I've always said that. Well, I can't stand here chatting with you, got a lot to do. And, by the by dear lad, I shouldn't like you to think that I was drunk.' He looked hard down at William and tweaked his ear. 'You're too young to know but there's worse things can happen to a man than a twisted foot, Billy, dear lad. I drink enough, but it's just enough and no more. Now you do as I say, go swimming. Once in the water you'll be the equal of anyone.'

'But I can't swim,' said William. 'My brothers can but I never learnt to. It's difficult for me to get down on the rocks.'

'Dear lad,' said Sam, brushing off his coat. 'If you can run with a foot like that, then you can most certainly swim. Mark my words, dear lad; I may look like an old soak – I know what they call me – but drink in moderation inspires great wisdom. Do as I say, get down to the sea and swim.'

*　*　*

William went down to the sea in secret that afternoon because he knew his mother would worry. Worse than that, she might try to stop him from going if she thought it was dangerous. She was busy in the kitchen so he said simply that he would make his own way across the fields to their rock and watch the kestrel they had seen the day before floating on the warm air high above the bracken. He had been to the seashore before of course, but always accompanied by his mother who had helped him down the cliff path to the beach below.

Swimming in the sea was forbidden. It was a family edict, and one observed by all the farming families around, whose respect and fear of the sea had been inculcated into them for generations. 'The sea is for fish,' his father had warned them often enough. 'Swim in the rock pools all you want, but don't go swimming in the sea.'

With his brothers and his father making hay in the high field by the chapel William knew there was little enough chance of his being discovered. He did indeed pause for a rest on the rock to look skywards for the kestrel, and this somehow eased his conscience. Certainly there was a great deal he had not told his mother, but he had never deliberately deceived her before this. He felt however such a strong compulsion to follow Sam's advice that he soon left the rock behind him and made for the cliff path. He was now further from home than he had ever been on his own before.

The cliff path was tortuous, difficult enough for anyone to negotiate with two good feet, but William managed well enough using a stick as a crutch to help him over the streams that tumbled down fern-green gorges to the sea below. At times he had to go down on all fours to be sure he would not slip. As he clambered up along the path to the first headland, he turned and looked back along the coast towards Zennor Head, breathing in the wind from the sea. A sudden wild feeling of exuberance and elation came over him so that he felt somehow liberated and at one with the world. He cupped his hands to his mouth and shouted to a tanker that was cruising motionless far out to sea:

'I'm Limping Billy Tregerthen,' he bellowed, 'and I'm going to swim. I'm going to swim in the sea. I can see you but you can't see me. Look out fish, here I come. Look out seals, here I come. I'm Limping Billy Tregerthen and I'm going to swim.'

So William came at last to Trevail Cliffs where the rocks step out into the sea but even at low tide never so far as to join the island. The island where the seals come lies some way off the shore, a black bastion against the sea, warning it that it must not come any further. Cormorants and shags perched on the island like sinister sentries and below them William saw the seals basking in the sun on the rocks. The path down to the beach was treacherous and William knew it. For the first time he had to manage on his own, so he sat down and bumped his way down the track to the beach.

He went first to the place his brothers had learnt to swim, a great green bowl of sea water left behind in the rocks by the tide. As he clambered laboriously over the limpet-covered rocks towards the pool, he remembered how he had sat alone high on the cliff top above and watched his brothers and his father diving and splashing in the pool below, and how his heart had filled with envy and longing. 'You sit there, with your Mother,' his father had said. 'It's too dangerous for you out there on those rocks. Too dangerous.'

'And here I am,' said William aloud as he stepped gingerly forward onto the next rock, reaching for a hand-hold to support himself. 'Here I am, leaping from rock to rock like a goat. If only they could see me now.'

He hauled himself up over the last lip of rock and there at last was the pool down below him, with the sea lapping in gently at one end. Here for the first time William began to be frightened. Until this moment he had not fully understood the step he was about to take. It was as if he had woken suddenly from a dream: the meeting with Sam in the hay-barn, his triumphant walk along the cliff path, and the long rock climb to the pool. But now as he looked around him he saw he was surrounded entirely by sea and stranded on the rocks a great distance out from the beach. He began to doubt if he could ever get back; and had it not been for the seal William would most certainly have turned and gone back home.

The seal surfaced silently into the pool from nowhere. William crouched down slowly so as not to alarm him and watched. He had never been this close to a seal. He had seen them often enough lying out on the rocks on the island like great grey cucumbers and had spotted their shining heads floating out at sea. But now he was so close he could see that the seal was looking directly at him out of sad, soulful eyes. He had never noticed before that seals had whiskers. William watched for a while and then spoke. It seemed rude not to.

'You're in my pool,' he said. 'I don't mind really, though I was going to have a swim. Tell you the truth, I was having second thoughts anyway, about the swimming I mean. It's all right for you, you're born to it. I mean you don't find getting around on land that easy, do you? Well nor do I. And that's why Sam told me to go and learn to swim, said I'd swim like a seal one day. But I'm a bit frightened, see. I don't know if I can, not with my foot.'

The seal had vanished as he was speaking, so William lowered himself carefully step by step down towards the edge of the pool. The water was clear to the bottom, but there was no sign of the seal. William found it reassuring to be able to see the bottom, a great slab of rock that fell away towards the opening to the sea. He could see now why his brothers had come here to learn, for one end of the pool was shallow enough to paddle whilst the other was so deep that the bottom was scarcely visible.

William undressed quickly and stepped into the pool, feeling for the rocks below with his toes. He drew back at the first touch because the water stung him with cold, but soon he had both feet in the water. He looked down to be sure of his footing, watching his feet move forward slowly out into the pool until he was waist-high. The cold had taken the breath from his body and he was tempted to turn around at once and get out. But he steeled himself, raised his hands above his head, sucked in his breath and inched his way forward. His feet seemed suddenly strange to him, apart from him almost and he wriggled his toes to be sure that they were still attached to him. It was then that he noticed that they had changed. They had turned white, dead white; and as William gazed down he saw that his left foot was no longer twisted. For the first time in his life his feet stood parallel. He was about to bend down to try to touch his feet, for he knew his eyes must surely be deceiving him, when the seal reappeared only a few feet away in the middle of the pool. This time the seal gazed at him only for a few brief moments and then began a series of water acrobatics that soon had William laughing and clapping with joy. He would dive, roll and twist, disappear for a few seconds and then materialise somewhere else. He circled William, turning over on his back and rolling, powering his way to the end of the pool before flopping over on his front and aiming straight for William like a torpedo, just under the surface. It was a display of comic elegance, of easy power. But to William it was more than this, it became an invitation he found he could not refuse.

The seal had settled again in the centre of the pool, his great wide eyes beckoning. William never even waited for the water to stop churning but launched himself out into the water. He sank of course, but he had not expected not to. He kicked out with his legs and failed his arms wildly in a supreme effort to regain the surface. He had sense enough to keep his mouth closed but his eyes were wide open and he saw through the green that the seal was swimming alongside him, close enough to touch. William knew that he was not drowning, that the seal would not let him drown; and with that confidence his arms and legs began to move more easily through the water. A few rhythmic strokes up towards the light and he found the air his lungs had been craving for. But the seal was nowhere to be seen. William struck out across to the rocks on the far side of the pool quite confident that the seal was still close by. Swimming came to William that day as it does to a dog. He found in that one afternoon the confidence to master the water. The seal however never reappeared, but William swam on now by himself until the water chilled his bones, seeking everywhere for the seal and calling for him. He thought of venturing out into the open ocean but thought better of it when he saw the swell outside the pool. He vowed he would come again, every day, until he found his seal.

William lay on the rocks above the pool, his eyes closed against the glare of the evening sun off the water, his heart still beating fast from the exertion of his swim. He lay like this, turning from time to time until he was dry all over. Occasionally he would laugh out loud in joyous celebration of the first triumph of his life. Out on the seal island the cormorants and shags were startled and lifted off the rocks to make for the fishing grounds out to sea, and the colony of seals was gathering as it always did each evening.

As William made his way back along the cliff path and up across the fields towards home he could hear behind him the soft hooting sound of the seals as they welcomed each new arrival on the rocks. His foot was indeed still twisted, but he walked erect now, the stoop gone from his shoulders and there was a new lightness in his step.

He broke the news to his family at supper that evening, dropped it like a bomb and it had just the effect he had expected and hoped for. They stopped eating and there was a long heavy silence whilst they looked at each other in stunned amazement.

'What did you say, Billy?' said his father sternly, putting down his knife and fork.

'I've been swimming with a seal,' William said,' and I learnt to swim just like Sam said. I climbed down to the rocks and I swam in the pool with the seal. I know we mustn't swim in the sea but the pool's all right isn't it?'

'By yourself, Billy?' said his mother, who had turned quite pale. 'You shouldn't have, you know, not by yourself. I could have gone with you.'

'It was all right, Mother,' William smiled up at her. 'The seal looked after me. I couldn't have drowned, not with him there.'

Up to that point it had all been predictable, but then his brothers began to laugh, spluttering about what a good tale it was and how they had actually believed him for a moment; and when William insisted that he could swim now, and that the seal had helped him, his father lost his patience. 'It's bad enough your going off on your own without telling your mother, but then you come back with a fantastic story like that and expect me to believe it. I'm not stupid lad. I know you can't climb over those rocks with a foot like that; and as for swimming and seals, well it's a nice story, but a story's a story, so let's hear no more of it.'

'But he was only exaggerating, dear,' said William's mother. 'He didn't mean . . .'

'I know what he meant,' said his father. 'And it's your fault, like as not, telling him all these wild stories and putting strange ideas in his head.'

William looked at his mother in total disbelief, numbed by the realisation that she too doubted him. She smiled sympathetically at him and came over to stroke his head.

'He's just exaggerating a bit, aren't you Billy?' she said gently.

But William pulled away from her embrace, hurt by her lack of faith.

'I don't care if you don't believe me,' he said, his eyes filling with tears. 'I know what happened. I can swim I tell you, and one day I'll swim away from here and never come back. I hate you, I hate you all.'

His defiance was punished immediately. He was sent up to his room and as he passed his father's chair he was cuffed roundly on the ear for good measure. That evening, as he lay on his bed in his pyjamas listening to the remorseless ker-thump, ker-thump of the haybaler outside in the fields, William made up his mind to leave home.

His mother came up with some cocoa later on as she always did, but he pretended to be asleep, even when she leant over and kissed him gently on the forehead.

'Don't be unhappy, Billy,' she said. 'I believe you, I really do.'

He was tempted at that moment to wake and to call the whole plan off, but resentment was still burning too strongly inside him. When it mattered she had not believed him, and even now he knew she was merely trying to console him. There could be no going back. He lay still and tried to contain the tears inside his eyes.

Every afternoon after school that week William went back down to the beach to swim. One of his brothers must have said something for word had gone round at school that 'Limping Billy' claimed that he had been swimming with the seals. He endured the barbed ridicule more patiently than ever because he knew that it would soon be over and he would never again have to face their quips and jibes, their crooked smiles.

The sea was the haven he longed for each day. The family were far too busy making hay to notice where he was and he was never to speak of it again to any of them.

To start with he kept to the green pool in the rocks. Every afternoon his seal would be there waiting for him and the lesson would begin. He learnt to roll in the water like a seal and to dive deep exploring the bottom of the pool for over a minute before surfacing for air. The seal teased him in the water, enticing him to chase, allowing William to come just so close before whisking away out of reach again. He learnt to lie on the water to rest as if he were on a bed, confident that his body would always float, that the water would always hold it up. Each day brought him new technique and new power in his legs and arms. Gradually the seal would let him come closer until one afternoon just before he left the pool William reached out slowly and stroked the seal on his side. It was gesture of love and thanks. The seal made no immediate attempt to move away but turned slowly in the water and let out a curious groan of acceptance before diving away out of the pool and into the open sea. As he watched him swim away, William was sure at last of his place in the world.

With the sea still calm next day William left the sanctuary of the pool and swam out into the swell of the ocean with the seal alongside him. There to welcome them as they neared the island were the bobbing heads of the entire seal colony. When they swam too fast for him it seemed the easiest, most natural thing in the world to throw his arms around the seal and hold on, riding him over the waves out towards the island. Once there he lay out on the rocks with them and was minutely inspected by each member of the colony. They came one by one and lay beside him, eyeing him wistfully before lumbering off to make room for the next. Each of them was different and he found he could tell at once the old from the young and the female from the male. Later, sitting cross-legged on the rocks and surrounded entirely by the inquisitive seals, William tasted raw fish for the first time, pulling away the flesh with his teeth as if he had been doing it all his life. He began to murmur seal noises in an attempt to thank them for their gift and they responded with great hoots of excitement and affection. By the time he was escorted back to the safety of the shore he could no longer doubt that he was one of them.

* * *

The notepad he left behind on his bed the next afternoon read simply: 'Gone to sea, where I belong.' His mother found it that evening when she came in from the fields at dusk. The Coastguard and the villagers were alerted and the search began. They searched the cliffs and the sea shore from Zennor Head to Wicca Pool and beyond, but in vain. An air-sea rescue helicopter flew low over the coast until the darkness drove it away. But the family returned to the search at first light and it was William's father who found the bundle of clothes hidden in the rocks below Trevail Cliffs. The pain was deep enough already, so he decided to tell no one of his discovery, but buried them himself in a corner of the cornfield below the chapel. He wept as he did so, as much out of remorse as for his son's lost life.

Some weeks later they held a memorial service in the church, attended by everyone in the village except Sam whom no one had seen since William's disappearance. The Parochial Church Council was inspired to offer a space on the church wall for a memorial tablet for William, and they offered to finance it themselves. It should be left to the family they said, to word it as they wished.

Months later Sam was hauling in his nets off Wicca Pool. The fishing had been poor and he expected his nets to be empty once again. But as he began hauling it was clear he had struck it rich and his heart rose in anticipation of a full catch at last. It took all his strength to pull the net up through the water. His arms ached as he strained to find the reserves he would need to haul it in. He had stopped hauling for a moment to regain his strength, his feet braced on the deck against the pitch and toss of the boat, when he heard a voice behind him.

'Sam,' it said, quietly.

He turned instantly, a chill of fear creeping up his spine. It was William Tregerthen, his head and shoulders showing above the gunwale of the boat.

'Billy?' said Sam. 'Billy Tregerthen? Is it you, dear lad? Are you real, Billy? Is it really you?' William smiled at him to reassure him. 'I've not had a drink since the day you died, Billy, honest I haven't. Told myself I never would again, not after what I did to you.' He screwed up his eyes. 'No,' he said, 'I must be dreaming. You're dead and drowned. I know you are.'

'I'm not dead and I'm not drowned, Sam,' William said. 'I'm living with the seals where I belong. You were right, Sam, right all along. I can swim like a seal, and I live like a seal. You can't limp in the water, Sam.'

'Are you really alive, dear lad?' said Sam. 'After all this time? You weren't drowned like they said?'

'I'm alive, Sam, and I want you to let your nets down,' William said. 'There's one of my seals caught up in it and there's no fish there I promise you. Let them down, Sam, please, before you hurt him.'

Sam let the nets go gently hand over hand until the weight was gone.

'Thank you Sam,' said William. 'You're a kind man, the only kind man I've ever known. Will you do something more for me?' Sam nodded, quite unable to speak any more. 'Will you tell my mother that I'm happy and well, that all her stories were true, and that she must never be sad. Tell her all is well with me. Promise?'

'Course,' Sam whispered. 'Course I will, dear lad.'

And then as suddenly as he had appeared, William

was gone. Sam called out to him again and again. He wanted confirmation, he wanted to be sure his eyes had not been deceiving him. But the sea around him was empty and he never saw him again.

William's mother was feeding the hens as she did every morning after the men had left the house. She saw Sam coming down the lane towards the house and turned away. It would be more sympathy and she had had enough of that since William died. But Sam called after her and so she had to turn to face him. They spoke together for only a few minutes, Sam with his hands on her shoulders, before they parted leaving her alone again with her hens clucking impatiently around her feet. If Sam had turned as he walked away he would have seen that she was smiling through her tears.

The inscription on the tablet in the church reads:

WILLIAM TREGERTHEN

AGED 10

Gone to sea, where he belongs

MILK FOR THE CAT

OLD MAN BARBERY HAD BEEN FARMING below the Eagle's Nest at Tremedda for as long as anyone in Zennor parish could remember. The wind and the years had gnarled his leathery face and bent his bones; but his sharp blue eyes, although watery with age, remained bright with joy until the end. He died as every man should die – in his sleep. He left no mark in the world except his son, and the farm at Tremedda which he had not altered in sixty years.

During the twilight of his life no one could

understand how he remained so smiling and contented, when so far as anyone else could see his life was and had been one long round of hard labour on the land and of wretched tragedy at home. He had married very late in life and his young wife had died in childbirth leaving him, already an old man, with an only son to bring up.

He was the wise old man of the village, and when asked, as he often was, how he stayed so cheerful, his eyes would smile and he would say:

'The secret is to be in tune with the land, to be in rhythm with the seasons, to rise with the sun and to go to bed as it sets. The land is like a god,' he would say, wagging his crooked finger. 'Love the land and it will love you in return.'

Thomas was still young when the old man died. For some years already he had worked on the land alongside his father, but always under his father's direction. There was a small herd of sundry milking cows still milked by hand in the old parlour below the house. The suckling cows and bullocks wintered out in amongst the rocks and the dead bracken. The dozen sows were still housed in a piggery that was so ancient that it looked as if it had sprung from the ground a millennium before. They had nearly a hundred lambing ewes each year and countless bedraggled hens and muddy ducks that wandered at will and laid whenever and wherever they found it convenient. A few fields were put to oats and barley, and there was always one field of potatoes. They had the machinery they needed for ploughing and harvesting, but always fourth-hand and rusty. 'Workable', his father called it. He would allow no weedkiller and no pesticides to be sprayed on his land – his father referred to them as 'damned blasphemies'.

Thomas had often pleaded with his old father to modernise, but the old man would always point out that they had money in the bank, didn't they, and that the land looked well, didn't it? 'Put all your eggs in one basket Thomas,' he would say, 'and then tell me what happens if you drop the basket.' There was no arguing with him, Thomas knew that and was a gentle enough person not to want to hurt an old man by persisting.

'You'll have your time, Thomas,' he had whispered urgently the day before he died, 'and when it comes you'll do what you must do: but I warn you Thomas, do not hurry the land, do not upset the balance. And remember the story; remember to leave out the bowl of milk each night as we have always done, and to leave the one row of potatoes in the ground every year. My father made them a promise and I've kept to it, and you must keep to it. Promise me that much.'

To others it might have sounded like the ramblings of a dying old man, but Thomas had grown up with the story and knew how important it was to his father.

'I promise Father,' he said. 'Of course I'll keep the promise.'

But the promise was made only to comfort his father. Once made, it was forgotten. In everything but this Thomas respected the wisdom of his father, although he may not always have agreed with him.

He had been brought up with the story that had first fascinated him and then stretched his credulity as a growing child, but that had become quite ridiculous to him now that he was a grown man. The farm, so his father said, was inhabited by a family of strange little folk – his father called them 'my little friends'. He himself had never seen one of them but his father before him had seen and spoken to them, indeed he had made a solemn bargain with them. On their part the little folk would guard the farm and all the animals, keeping them free from disease and misfortune; and on his part the farmer would treat the land with the love and respect it deserved; and to seal the bargain the family would supply the little folk with milk and potatoes for ever and ever. Accordingly, each evening after milking, for over a hundred years now a bowl of fresh warm milk had been put out on the rock in the meadow below the cowshed. And each year a long line of potatoes was left in the ground after harvest, and when it was ploughed up the next spring there was never a potato to be found.

As a child Thomas loved the story and longed for his father to set him on his knee by the stove and tell it to him again and again; and when he grew up he heard of other similar legends of strange little people on other farms and up on the moors by the Quoit – but by this time they were mere legends to be enjoyed, but not to be believed. He had long since stopped lying low in the grass to ambush one of the little folk. He no longer put his ear to the rocks to listen in on their conversations.

So with his father dead and buried, Thomas now began to make changes at Tremedda Farm. With the money so carefully saved up over the years by his father he built a magnificent herring-bone milking parlour and installed a huge silver bulk tank. He trebled the size of the milking herd in the first year and worked like a slave to himself to finance the modernisation of the piggery and the building of a covered yard for the bullocks and suckling cows. He bulldozed away the hedgerows, the boulders and the giant fuchsias to enlarge the fields so he could farm more efficiently. He began to spray the encroaching bracken instead of burning it as his father had done.

Within a few short years the farm was transformed out of all recognition. His hard work and his success were admired all over Penwith; and he soon found himself a wife and brought her back to live with him at Tremedda. She loved the peace of the place and the feeling of being at the end of the earth, and they were happy. Thomas wanted his first child to be a boy so that he could take on the farm after him, and sure enough the boy came, healthy and strong. The world seemed truly to have become his oyster, but in all that time he had not once put out the bowl of milk and he no longer even grew a field of potatoes. It was not economic to grow just a few potatoes, and anyway he needed all the land to supply the barley and the straw he needed for the cows. So there was no room any more for potatoes, but even if he had grown potatoes he certainly would never have left them to rot in the ground for the sake of a ridiculous legend.

One summer evening Thomas finished the milking as usual and drove the cows out into the fields. He stood for a moment in his waterproof apron surveying the cows as they meandered out towards the sunset that had turned the still sea into a lake of red gold. He was a completely happy and fulfilled man at that moment, proud of his smart black-and-white milkers. With a sense of deep satisfaction he surveyed his land that stretched from the moor to the sea and back along the fields towards the village, and then feeling considerably proprietary he undid his apron and made his way back to the milking parlour.

Had he not held on to the handle of the dairy door

as he opened it he would certainly have fallen over in astonishment, for seated cross-legged on his silver bulk tank was a little wrinkled old man, with fly-away grey hair and wide wild eyes and twitching eyebrows.

'Good evening, Thomas Barbery,' he said in a strangely youthful voice that was as kind as his smile.

Thomas was not one to doubt the evidence of his eyes, nor was he by nature either fearful or nervous; but he was now shocked into a state of such disbelief that he could find no words to answer the apparition on the bulk tank.

'I see you've lost your tongue. Thomas Barbery,' the little old man went on, still smiling. 'I won't harm you – we're not like that, not at all, not at all. You see, Thomas, we're here to help you – we always have been only you didn't want to believe it. All we want from you is a little consideration and kindness, so that we can live happily alongside each other.'

'Who are you?' Thomas asked, finally finding the nerve to speak out. 'Who are you and what do you want from me?'

'Questions must have answers,' said the old man

springing down lightly from the bulk tank to the ground and wiping his hands on the back of his serge trousers. He would not stop smiling. 'Perhaps I should introduce myself – it's only polite. I knew your grandfather and your grandfather knew me. I knew your father and your father knew me, even though he never met me. But I'm quite sure he told you about us, and about our little arrangement. Yes, I can see he did, and I can see you didn't believe him, did you? We're the little people – I believe you call us knockers or pixies or boggarts, or what have you. All we do is to look after the countryside, to make sure that farms are properly cared for and that the animals are happy. In return all we ask is a bowl of milk each evening and a line of potatoes each year – we love potatoes. You may not have seen us before but we live here just as you do and we need food. Thomas Barbery, you've given us no milk and no potatoes since the day your good father died. And we've been watching you, watching you tearing the heart out of the farm with all your new buildings and your bulldozers, punishing the land and sucking it dry. We can take just so much Thomas Barbery, but when we saw that you were beginning to poison the countryside with all your insecticides and your pesticides, and spraying the land with your weedkillers, well that was the final straw. You have broken the ancient agreement between your grandfather and the little people and I've come to ask you, to beg you to mend your ways before it is too late. In future Thomas Barbery, you must take from the land only as much as you put in. You must love the land. It's what your father taught you. From now on you must restore our daily bowl of milk from the dairy and our line of potatoes – it's not much to ask is it?'

During this speech which was delivered with great passion and with expansive gestures, Thomas had regained his composure. Perhaps it was because he could now look down on the little old man who stood after all no higher than his knees, or perhaps it was the permanent, gentle smile on his wizened face that reassured Thomas and gave him the confidence to speak out boldly.

There was anger and resentment in his voice.

'You may have frightened my grandfather into this agreement,' he said, 'but you'll not frighten me. I am master of my own land. It is my land. No one, no one tells me how to run my own farm. It is mine and I shall do with it as I wish. As for the milk and potatoes – you can sing for them, for you'll have none of mine.'

'Oh dear, oh dear, oh dear,' said the old man, walking slowly towards the door, shaking his head all the while. 'You don't understand do you, do you Thomas Barbery? The land belongs to no one. Not to you and not to me. We borrow it for a lifetime – that's all – and then we hand it on to those who come after us.'

He turned and faced Thomas and looked hard into his eyes.

'I don't wish to harm you, you must believe that. But if you will not keep to our ancient agreement, then we on our part will no longer protect your farm and your animals, and you'll be on your own.'

'Go away old man,' Thomas shouted, pointing to the door and advancing towards him. 'I don't need you. Go home and tell your little friends that there's no place here for redundant knockers.'

'That's a pity, Thomas Barbery,' said the little old man, pulling up the collar of his tattered jacket, his face wreathed in the same kindly smile. 'A terrible pity. I'll be back.'

And he went out into the evening light.

'Getting colder; autumn's on the way again,' he said almost to himself. 'Goodbye Thomas Barbery.'

And he was gone.

Of course Thomas never spoke of this meeting to anyone for fear of being ridiculed; he even kept it a secret from his wife, and after a few weeks had gone he barely believed his own memory of it. He was soon wrapped up again in the daily routine of work on the farm and had little time to reflect on this strange encounter. He made a conscious effort too to forget the incident, for deep down it troubled him greatly and he did not want to think of it.

The autumn fog came rolling in now each evening to blot out the sun, and the heather and the bracken faded on the moor above Tremedda. The sea turned winter grey beyond the ploughed fields, and the wind whipped across the fields from the open sea bringing with it the first storms of winter. The cows were driven into their winter quarters in the yard behind the parlour. They would not see the grass again until spring.

Quite soon after the first frost it became apparent to Thomas that the milk yield was falling. Of course it fell anyway in the winter months but it was falling unusually fast. He put this down at first to the driving rain and the cold, and to the poor quality of the hay he had cut that summer. But no matter how much sugar-beet and barley he fed to his cows to compensate, he could not stop the slide. Cows were drying off before their time, and even those in the full flush of milk seemed to carry half empty udders. Each evening the milk level in the bulk tank was falling perceptibly lower, and at last Thomas acknowledged to himself that he had a problem. He called out the vet time after time to examine the cows, but the vet shook his head and whistled through his teeth declaring himself perplexed. All he could do was to prescribe a dose of minerals and vitamins. It seemed for a time that this might work, but very soon the level in the tank fell yet again.

Sick with anxiety, for the milk was his main winter income from the farm, Thomas lay awake each night and worried. One wet November night Thomas was lying in bed in the early hours listening to the rain against the window pane when it came to him that there could be a fox prowling in the yard, frightening the cows, or perhaps even it was rats that were upsetting them. He threw on his old raincoat and went out into the wet black of the night. He took his gun with him just in case. As he opened the yard gate he heard quite clearly the sound of sucking, and that was strange for the suckling cows were housed a long way away in the new sheds by the covered yard. Even so he imagined at first that the wind must be carrying the sound across the fields from the covered yard – that was the only reasonable explanation. It was only when he shone his torch along the long line of cubicles that he discovered the cause of the sucking sound, for every cow in the herd was sucking hard on her own udder. He ran along the shed shouting at them to stop, but they paid him no attention.

'It's no use, Thomas Barbery,' said a soft voice behind him, a voice he recognised only too well. 'Once they've tasted it it's the devil to stop them you know.

Takes them back to their calfhood I suppose.'

Of course Thomas knew before he turned around to whom the voice belonged, but he shone his torch in the direction of the voice just to be sure. The little old man stood watching him, leaning on his elbow against the yard wall.

'A pity, Thomas Barbery, what a terrible pity, but these things happen in farming you know.'

And he turned around and vanished into the night before Thomas had recovered sufficiently to raise his gun, or even to think about doing so.

Gales came in January as they always did, howling in from the Atlantic, and seeking in their fury to tear every building from its foundations. The great hay barn behind the covered yard that had stood the test for a hundred years and more, shook and rattled until the new corrugated iron roof flew off one night bit by bit and clattered down into the yard. The storm lasted for forty-eight hours so there was no possibility of saving the hay. Thomas and his wife tried in vain to haul a great tarpaulin over the exposed stack, but the force of the wind whipped it from their hands and they soon had to give up the unequal struggle. By the time the rain subsided and the wind blew itself out, every bale of hay and straw in the stack was saturated.

Thomas stood in the wreck of his barn and would have wept like a child, but a great anger raged in his heart and held back his tears.

'A pity, Thomas Barbery,' came a sympathetic voice from high up in the haystack above him. 'A terrible pity, but these things happen in farming you know.'

In his fury Thomas bent and picked up a stone and sent if flying up towards the little old man, but he had vanished.

'Go to the devil,' he shouted. 'I know what you're up to and I'll never give in. I won't believe in fairy stories.'

Some of the hay and straw was retrievable, but even that never lost the smell of damp and the mildew set in to spoil all but a few hundred bales. So there was a new roof to be paid for and ten thousand bales of hay and straw to buy in, enough to feed and bed the stock through to the end of the winter. And still the cows were sucking themselves as they lay in the cubicles.

When the ewes began to lamb in February and there

were twins and even triplets born daily out in the high fields by the cliffs, Thomas' spirits rose with a fresh hope. The spring came back in his step and he was, his wife noticed, his old self once again. The perpetual glower and heavy silence she had known in the last few months disappeared. Day after day he would come back into the house for breakfast, his face red from the biting wind, and report triumphantly that more doubles and triples had been born over night and that all the lambs were strong and healthy. This success enabled Thomas to shake off the problems of the milking herd and the hay barn. It was the heaviest crop of lambs ever bred on the farm – a reward he thought for his new policy of breeding only from the most commercial breeds of lowland sheep. The success however was to prove shortlived.

Lambing was almost over and they were into a mild spell at the end of the month when the deadly white-scour struck the flock. One by one the lambs weakened and went off their legs, and now when he came back for his breakfast each morning he carried at least one dead lamb in each hand. In desperation he brought the whole flock inside to keep a closer eye on them and injected every lamb, but this seemed merely to accelerate the spread of the disease. Within a week he lost over fifty lambs before he took his vet's advice and moved the sheep out onto the hills again. Then just as suddenly as it had begun the disease vanished.

He was burying the last of the dead lambs in the soft hillside under Tregarthen cottages when he felt a presence behind him, and there, sitting up on an ivy covered rock, was the little old man. Sadness was etched on his face and the smile that was always there was a smile of sympathy.

'A pity, Thomas Barbery,' he said shaking his head. 'A terrible pity, but these things happen in farming you know.'

He hopped down from the rock and walked towards him.

'Thomas Barbery,' he said, 'we want to help you. You've only to ask us. Please let us help you.'

But Thomas could not bring himself to reply. He felt dejected and demoralised, but his pride refused to allow him to speak. He ignored his visitor and bent once again to dig the shallow graves, reflecting grimly on his growing catalogue of misfortune.

Thomas had a particular pride in his calves, but shut up as they were all winter in the sheds and the covered yard, they began to develop ringworm. The great crusty growths crowded their faces and ran down their necks. It spread from one to the other until every beast in the covered yard was infected. Once again the vet was called in to treat them, but with no success, and much against his own better judgement Thomas called in an old farmer friend of his father's from Morvah to charm the ring-worm away. But neither magic nor medicine had any effect. In the market his farmer friends, who loved always to find fault, pointed out that his sheds probably needed a good cleaning out, and one or two mentioned that cattle were always healthier if they wintered out.

The tidal wave of misery was gathering momentum by the week. A farrowing sow lay on her litter and squashed half of them, a bullock broke into the granary one night and gorged itself to death on cattle nuts, and in the muggy March mists Thomas lost three calves with viral pneumonia. Then the hens began quite unaccountably to cannibalise their own eggs. And still the cows were not milking as they should and the hay and straw had to be paid for as well as the barn roof, and all his calves were covered in ringworm. Then there were the dead lambs – he could not forget the lambs.

Thomas always hayed up his suckling cows in the covered yard last thing at night after the milking. He had finished and was spreading straw behind them for their bedding when he heard a cough. He thought it was a cow at first, but when he looked up he saw it was no cow.

'A pity Thomas, a terrible pity.'

The little old man was sitting cross-legged up on the hayrack and smiling gently as he always did. It was not the smile of triumph – even Thomas could see that.

The tone of his voice was gentle, not gloating.

'These things happen in farming you know. It's not your fault – none of it is your fault. None of it is our fault either – we don't make these things happen. We are not happy that you are unhappy – believe me Thomas. Let us help you, Thomas, let us talk like friends. We have to be friends sooner or later. The story your father told you was true, Thomas. Why should he tell you a lie? Was he a foolish man? Was he a stupid farmer? Was he a bad father? Let's strike a bargain and we'll all go to work and help put things to rights again. We'll work together, just like I did with your father and with his father before him. What do you say Thomas?'

But Thomas said nothing. He simply strode out of the building and banged the steel doors closed behind him. He was consumed with such a deep sense of hurt and humiliation that he could not even bring himself to look at the little old man as he passed him.

As his farming fortunes deteriorated, his unhappiness spilled over at home. He was sharp now with his wife where before he had been gentle and kind, and he had no time for his toddling son who would coo plaintively at his brooding father to try to get him to play as he used to. Any wandering sheep or cattle were a cause for unreasoning dispute with his farming friends and neighbours who scarcely recognised him these days as the Thomas Barbery they had known since schooldays. Sympathy or kindness on their part seemed to arouse only a sullen resentment so that as time passed there were very few offers of help. No one could reach him, not even his wife, who lived her life now in perpetual dread of his black moods. The prospect of ruin had settled on him and cast a shadow not only over him but over everyone who knew him and loved him.

There is no mains water serving the farms that run along the cliff tops at Zennor. Tremedda farm, like the others, is fed by a spring that bubbles up into a leat below the Eagle's Nest. There had always been more than enough water for the farm and for the house. No-one could ever remember the water at Tremedda running dry. Even in drought years when there is no water left in the reservoirs and the wells run dry all over Penwith, the leat below the Eagle's Nest flows strong and plentifully, and the troughs in the fields are always full. So when one morning in early spring the water to the drinking-troughs in the cowyard suddenly stopped and the taps in the house ran dry, Thomas could only imagine that there was a blockage in the pipe. But try as he did to unblock it, not a dribble of water trickled out of the pipe. With increasing anxiety he climbed up the rocks through the gorse to the leat on the hillside and found it empty.

Thomas sat down on a great flat slab of granite, numb with despair, and looked out over his farm. Without water there could be no farm – he knew that well enough. He could hear the thunder of the sea against the cliffs and the urgent mooing of his thirsty cattle. The first cuckoo called out from the woods by the old chapel ruin and he noticed that the daffodils that filled the garden of the ruined cottage nearby were in full flower. That, he remembered, was his favourite playing place as a child. The farm lay spread out below him. He could see his wife picking daffodils in the garden, and his son pedalling frantically round the sandpit on his tricycle. Thomas had not cried since he was a child, but tears came now to his eyes as he watched them. And then the cuckoo called again, a clear recurring call from the ruined cottage this time, a clearer call, more insistent.

'You're right,' he said aloud, wiping his eyes with the back of his hand and getting to his feet. 'I have been a cuckoo, a right cuckoo, and there's only one way I know to put things right.'

After milking that evening Thomas washed out his

father's old white bowl which he had kept in the corner of the dairy, and dipped it into the swirling milk in the tank. He walked out over the field towards the great rock in the meadow and set the bowl down in the centre of it before turning away and going back into the dairy to fetch the sack of potatoes he had brought down from the house. As he opened the door he was half expecting the little old man to be there, and indeed he was, sitting on the silver tank, his little legs crossed as Thomas had first seen him all those months before. They looked at each other for a moment before Thomas spoke.

'I need your help,' he said. 'I've put your milk out on the rock, and I'll let you have these potatoes to be going on with. There'll be a row for you and yours next year, I promise, and every year after that.'

The little old man's smile widened and he chuckled with delight, holding out his hand to Thomas, who took it gratefully and helped him to the ground.

'Thank you Thomas Barbery,' said the little old man. 'I knew we would be friends one day. From now on we will see to it that your farm and your family prospers.

Come on now,' and he reached up and took Thomas's hand, 'I've something to show you.'

He led Thomas by the hand out into the meadow and stood for a moment looking around him.

'It is beautiful,' he said. 'Is there any place more beautiful on all the earth?'

'No,' said Thomas. 'Come to think of it, I shouldn't think there is.'

'Watch this, Thomas Barbery,' the little man said, and he clapped his hands loudly three times. From under every rock on the farm it seemed, from the daffodil cottage and from the ruined chapel beyond came an army of little men and little women, running and jumping and capering until they gathered in a circle around the rock where they joined hands and danced together. 'You see,' said the little man. 'There's a lot of us, and now we're back at work we'll soon have your farm working just as it used to. We'll have a word with your cows right away and they'll stop their nonsense – you can be sure of that. You'll never see us again Thomas, not if you love the land and are true to us, but you'll always know we're there. And after you're gone we will look after your son, and his son after him when they take on the farm at Tremedda.'

In the months and the years that followed the farm thrived as it had never done before, and Thomas was a happy man again. Every evening since that terrible day when the leat below the Eagle's Nest unaccountably dried up, he put out the bowl of milk for the little people and he always grew a line of potatoes and left them in the land for his little friends.

When some time later his son asked him why he left out a bowl of milk every night on the great rock in the meadow below the milking parlour, he replied,

'It's for the cat. It's milk for the cat.'

'But we haven't got a cat, Father,' said the little boy.

'I know,' said Thomas, 'but for the moment let's pretend we have. When you're a bit older I'll tell you a story, a true story; and then you'll know why. But I'm not going to tell you just yet because you'd believe me, and if you believe it now you won't believe it later when it really matters.'

'I don't understand, Father,' said the little boy.

'You will, my lad,' said Thomas, and smiled to himself. 'You will.'

MAD MISS MARNEY

THERE IS A LOST HOUSE HIGH UP ON THE moor above Zennor churchtown where no one comes and no one goes. No road leads up to it, and even the peat-black track passes by the front gate as if it might be afraid to go any closer. It looks as if no one lives there for no curtain ever shivers and no smoke breathes out of the chimney. But someone does live there.

Mad Miss Marney has lived on her own up there for as many long years as anyone can remember. In all that time the only people she has ever spoken to are the shopkeepers in Penzance where she goes just a few times a year for provisions. On these rare appearances she is always a source of great interest and speculation for she goes dressed in a coat made from corn-sacks and tied around the waist with binder-cord. She talks to herself incessantly and cackles whenever she laughs. All this may well be why she is known as 'Mad Miss Marney'. Most people try to avoid her for she is disturbingly strange to look at, but for those who do take the time to speak to her she always has a toothy smile and an infectious laugh that often breaks into a high-pitched cackle.

To the children she is of course a witch. Any bent old lady who lives on her own, carries a knobbly walking stick and cackles when she laughs has to be a witch. But Mad Miss Marney is a witch mostly because the children have all been told to stay away from her by parents who themselves believe that there must be more to Mad Miss Marney than meets the eye.

One of these children was Kate Trelochie who unlike most children had no fear of the dark or of witches or of anything much, but like most children she was insatiably inquisitive. She lived at Wicca Farm under the shadow of the Eagle's Nest. She was an only child whose parents were so yoked to their farm and so consumed by the work of it that they had little time or energy to spare for their child. So she grew up a wild, independent soul wandering the fields and the cliffs with her friends, but always reserving the high moor by the Eagle's Nest for herself alone. The moor suited her for she was a creature of impulsive moods, at one moment unable to contain her exhilaration and at the next so full of despondency and gloom that she could scarcely speak to anyone. Ever since she could remember she had been drawn to the sighing mists and the whispering wilderness of the moor; everything from the collapsed three-legged Quoit, that last sad reminder of some ancient chieftain's earthly sway, to the great granite cheesewring rocks that overlooked Zennor itself – everything was her own private sanctuary, her kingdom.

She loved to be alone up there, to roam free over her kingdom with the wind tearing at her hair. She resented any intrusion – they had no right to be there, it was her place. Leaving the hoof-marked track behind her she would hurdle through the rough heather and clamber over the rocks until her legs would carry her no further. Then she would lie down on the soft spongy grass under the lee of a great boulder and close her eyes and listen to the secret sounds of the moor that spoke only to her – the distant cry of the gulls at sea, the bark of a wandering vixen and the mewing of the pair of buzzards that circled above her.

There was a part of Kate Trelochie that was indeed romantic and dreamy, but the other part was fiercely practical. She came to the high moor by the Eagle's Nest for a specific purpose as well, to hunt and capture specimens for her collection. When she had first come home some years before with a slow-worm wrapped around her wrist, her mother had screamed hysterically and banished all 'creepy-crawlies' from the house. But Kate wanted her slow-worm to be warm, and so she kept it secretly down at the bottom of her bed. Other creatures soon joined it in her bedroom: lizards, frogs, toads and even a grass snake. But when the grass snake escaped from his box and ate the frogs, she finally decided that her bedroom was not the place for her collection. So she took over the disused greenhouse at the bottom of the garden and set up her 'creepy-crawly' collection and opened it up to her friends – for a price. It was two pence a visit and an extra penny if you wanted to handle the grass snake. She made enough money from the proceeds to buy the nails and the wood and the glass she needed to repair the cages and the greenhouse itself. And she would keep her regular customers happy by bringing back new exhibits from her expeditions on the moor – anything from a mammoth stag beetle to a baby rabbit. The greenhouse came to be known to all the other children as Kate Trelochie's Zoo.

Her mother and father were quite happy about it for it kept her busy and out of mischief, or so they thought. Anyway they admired the entrepreneur in her, setting up on her own like that. They had only one repeated warning, that she was never to go near the lost house on the moor and she was never to talk to Mad Miss Marney.

'She's a strange one,' Kate's mother always said. 'Just like her mother was, from what they say. And of course you never know with people like that. It runs in the family. You never know. Just keep away from her, that's all.'

Kate had always been intrigued by the lost house and she longed to catch just a glimpse of Mad Miss Marney. Every time she passed the house she would pause and look for signs of life, but the place always looked deserted and empty. She thought often enough about climbing over the fence and snooping around the back of the house, but she thought that that would be wrong – it was private after all. What she needed was an excuse to go and knock on the door; so when just such a chance presented itself, she took it eagerly.

She had spent a long summer's afternoon on the moor trying to catch lizards as they basked on the rocks, but with no success for they were always too quick for her. So she was down-hearted and cross with herself as she began the long walk home down across the moor. She was crossing the track just below the lost house when she noticed something shiny on the dry black soil of the track. As she looked it moved and flapped to life. She froze where she stood and then crept closer. Whether it was a rook or a crow or a raven she was not sure; but it was lying on its side and trying desperately to move away from her using its wings as legs. But the effort of it was too much and the bird keeled over and lay still. It struggled only feebly as Kate picked it up and cradled it to her chest. Angry black eyes glared up at her as she stroked the glistening feathers on the top of its head. She stood for a moment wondering what she should do; and then she felt the blood sticky on her hand. Mad Miss Marney's house was close by and she had the perfect reason to knock on the door – she knew she had to find help if the bird was to live.

The door of the house opened before she had time to knock and standing in front of her was Mad Miss Marney, and at once Kate regretted her boldness for Miss Marney looked anything but pleased to see her.

'What do you want?' she said in a rasping voice. 'I've had children up here before coming knocking on my door and running away before I even get there. But I saw you coming up the path, so you haven't got time to run, have you? What d'you want?'

Taken aback, Kate held out the bird almost in self-defence.

'I found this,' she said. 'And I don't know what to do because it's bleeding. I think it's been shot or something. It can hardly move, but I thought you might be able to help. Sorry if I bothered you.'

She was a tiny bent old lady, hardly taller than Kate herself. She leant heavily on her stick and Kate noticed that her finger joints were all swollen and twisted. Her hair, a whispy silvery-white was pulled up in a bun on her head and the skin around her lips was puckered with age.

'People are always shooting,' said Miss Marney. 'The things people do for a bit of fun. Don't understand people. Never have done. Come on in child. Bring it in, bring it in. Don't just stand there. I'm not about to turn you into gingerbread. I would but I don't like it – can't take sweet things any more.'

Kate followed her into the house, looking around her as she went. There were books everywhere. The very walls seemed to be made of books. They stood now in the kitchen, and here too there were books instead of plates on the Welsh dresser.

'Well, what did you expect child, cauldrons and black cats, pointed hats and broomsticks?'

'No Miss Marney, honest,' Kate lied, and then she changed the subject quickly. 'It's bigger than I thought it would be inside, the house I mean. And I've never seen so many books in all my life.'

Miss Marney put the bird down on its back on the kitchen table. She spread the wings open.

'It's one of my ravens,' she said, almost in a whisper. There was a tremor in her voice. 'Jasper I think it is. Yes it is Jasper, full of gunshot – poor old thing.'

'Jasper?' Kate said.

'I give them all names,' Miss Marney said, walking slowly past her to put the kettle on the stove. She rolled back her sleeves and washed her hands carefully. 'Every bird, every creature on the moor. They are all my friends. I know every one of them – even the ones you take away.'

'You've seen me?' Kate was angry at the thought of it. 'You've been watching me?'

Miss Marney smiled for the first time – she had very few teeth.

'An old lady can look out of her window, can't she?' she said. 'Course I've been watching you, been watching you for years. After all you come up here more than anyone else and you always have a good look at my house, don't you?'

'But I don't hurt them,' Kate protested. 'I don't hurt the animals, I just keep them at home and look after them. They're for my collection, for my zoo that I've got in my greenhouse. D'you mind, Miss Marney?'

'No, not if you look after them,' Miss Marney said. 'Is Jasper for your collection as well, or did you just want to get a look inside the house and see if the old witch is as mad as everyone says?'

Kate was not quick enough to deny it. Miss Marney always seemed to be one step ahead of her and Kate was not used to that.

'I'll look after Jasper,' said Miss Marney. 'He'll be fine with me. You can come back tomorrow to pick him up if he's well enough and then you can look after him until he gets better. Would you like to do that? It'll be a month or two before he's fit to fly again. But you must let him go when he's better. He won't want to be shut up in a cage for the rest of his life.'

'Do you think he'll live?' Kate asked. 'He looks so

weak, and he must have lost a lot of blood.'

'Oh he'll live, child,' Miss Marney said bustling her towards the door. 'Jasper will live. I have my ways you know. There's not a lot I can't cure if I put my mind to it. Now off you go Kate, and come back tomorrow.'

'But how do you know my name, Miss Marney?' Kate asked, turning by the front door and facing the old lady.

Mad Miss Marney began to chortle and then broke into her witchy cackle.

'Thought you'd want to know that,' she said. 'I'm not the only one that talks to herself around here. I've heard you talking to yourself up here in the mist. You should be more careful. Voices carry a long way up on the moor. "Kate Trelochie," you said one day, only a few weeks back I remember. "Kate Trelochie, you're a genius, a genuine genius. Who else do you know who is only ten years old and has a zoo of her very own?" So you see we are two of a kind you and I. We are mad as hatters Kate. We love all God's creatures and we love this place with a passion no-one else would understand. You are the first person I've had in my house for fifty years and more.' She seemed anxious all of a sudden and leant closer to

Kate. 'You won't tell anyone you've met me will you?' Kate shook her head vigorously. 'I don't like people. Don't understand them, and they don't understand me. It's our secret then, just between the two of us.'

'Course, Miss Marney,' said Kate, and the old lady patted her on the head and went indoors.

It was a difficult promise to keep that evening with the zoo open as usual and all her friends around her. She longed to tell them all about Miss Marney and her amazing house of books, and she would have done but for a powerful feeling of affection for the old lady. She had been welcomed into a house where no other person had gone in fifty years, and she had been trusted by the old lady to keep their meeting a secret. Tempted as she was she could not and would not tell anyone, but she did go so far as to promise that tomorrow she might have a very special new attraction in the zoo.

'Where will you get it from?' they asked.

'What is it?'

'Can we pick it up like the grass snake?'

'Aha,' she said mysteriously to everyone. She knew she had said enough to bring them all back the next day with money in their pockets and so she said no more.

'I saw you up on the moor again this afternoon,' said her father that evening after supper. 'See you a mile off clambering around in that yellow shirt of yours. Find what you were looking for?'

'Sort of, Father,' she said and she smiled to herself.

'Nowhere near that house was she?' her mother asked sharply.

But to Kate's great relief no reply came from her father who was hidden again behind his newspaper.

'You keep away from there like I told you,' said her mother. 'From what I hear, and I wouldn't be surprised, there's some people say she's a witch.'

'I don't believe in witches,' said Kate.

'Never you mind what you believe in,' said her mother. 'You just mind what I say. There's things I could tell you my girl.'

The next morning she was up at first light to prepare a home for Jasper in the old stable that no one used any more. The greenhouse was already over-crowded and anyway she knew enough to know that Jasper and her creepy crawlies would not get on together. She cleared out the old rusty chains and plough shares, the rotten corn sacks and fertiliser bags, and swept it all clean. The hay-rack would make a perfect perch for Jasper when he was better and he would have room to spread his wings. Meanwhile she made a mattress of soft hay for Jasper to lie on.

The mist had come down again as she climbed up into the clouds towards the lost house. Even before she knocked on the front door she heard the old lady talking and laughing to herself at the back of the house.

'Come in, Kate,' she heard, and so she pushed open the door and went through into the kitchen.

Miss Marney was sitting in her rocking chair by the stove and sitting on her shoulder was Jasper who cawed unpleasantly at Kate as she came closer. Kate stood astonished. She could see no trace of his wounds. He seemed totally recovered.

'Don't mind him Kate, it's only talk. Come in, come in – he won't hurt. You didn't tell anyone you'd been up here did you?'

'No, Miss Marney,' Kate said quite unable to take her

eyes off Jasper. 'But I don't understand,' she said. 'He was almost dead yesterday. How do you do it?'

'Almost dead, but not quite,' said the old lady. 'He'll need some care, some rest and some good food – meat mind you. He likes his meat, don't you Jasper? Then he'll be righter than rain in a few weeks.'

'But how did you do it, Miss Marney?' Kate asked reaching out cautiously to smooth Jasper on the head.

'Oh, I have my ways,' Miss Marney said chortling. 'I have my ways. I'm quite pleased with him really. To be honest with you I was quite worried when you brought him in, but there's not a lot I can't do if I put my mind to it. Would you have a cup of tea, child? I've only one cup. I've only ever had need for one cup, you understand. But I've had mine so I'll wash it up and let you have a fresh cup. Jasper will go to you, won't you Jasper? He can't fly yet, so come a little closer so that he can hop onto your shoulder. That's right.' The raven put its head on one side and looked warily at Kate, who looked back just as warily. 'Go on Jasper, don't be silly,' said the old lady and she jerked her shoulder to get him to move, and Jasper hopped obediently across onto Kate's shoulder.

'Quite a weight, isn't he?' said Miss Marney. Tea won't be long. I've got the kettle on the boil.'

With Jasper balanced on her shoulder, Kate sipped her sweet strong tea and listened intently to the old lady as she sat back, rocking gently in her chair and talked and talked. It seemed as if she was making up for all those fifty years in which she had spoken to no-one. She talked of all her animal friends on the moor and of her beloved books. She had read every one of them several times over. She dreaded the cold of the winters she told Kate, for there was never enough money to heat the room and keep the damp away from her bones and the mildew away from her books. Her greatest desire in the world, she said, was for a great warm woolly coat and a hat to cover her ears. Every question that Kate wanted to ask she answered before she could even ask it. Miss Marney was a writer, she said, not a good writer, but not a bad one either. She wrote stories about all the people who lived below the Eagle's Nest, about all the farms she could see from her house, and about the animals and the birds and of course about her moor. But no one would ever read them, she said, because no one would believe them. 'They would think they are just made-up stories, but everything I write I have seen with my own eye, my mind's eye perhaps, but I see it just as clear as day.'

Several cups of tea later Kate felt she knew and loved the old lady better than anyone else in the whole world, but one thing still troubled her about Miss Marney.

'Miss Marney,' she said. 'It's about the bird . . .?'

'Jasper,' said the old lady smiling. 'Jasper. You must call him by his name – it's only polite you know. All right Kate, I know what you want to know. And you are my friend so you shall know. But you must never tell anyone what I am about to tell you for it is something that people do not understand, and what people cannot understand they fear, and when they fear they hate.' She sat back in her rocking chair and sighed sadly. 'I have a gift,' she said. 'I do not know where it comes from, but I have the gift of healing.'

'You mean,' said Kate, 'you mean that you can heal anything you want to? Then what they say is true, you are a kind of witch, a good witch.'

The old lady's eyes were closed and she nodded.

'I suppose so,' she said quietly. 'If it lives I can heal it, that's all there is to it. So now you know my secret. Guard it well my little friend, for if anyone were ever to find out that Mad Miss Marney really did have strange powers, then you know what they'd do, don't you?'

'No, Miss Marney,' said Kate.

'They'd put me away, Kate, like they did to my old mother. She had strange powers and they didn't like it so they sent her to a home and she never came back to me. That's why I have never trusted anyone before, why I have never told anyone of my gift, except you. And that's why no one else must ever know.'

It was a slow walk back over the moor with Jasper perched heavily on her shoulder. The warm sun had dispersed the mist and the sea was there again. As Kate came down the track towards home she could see that her usual customers were already waiting outside the greenhouse. She managed to dodge around the back of the house without being seen and lifted Jasper up onto his perch before going down to the bottom of the garden to face her clamouring friends outside the greenhouse. She took their money and put it in the biscuit-tin she used for a bank and then led them back into the stable-yard.

Once outside the stable with her back to the door she proudly introduced her new exhibit.

'He's the biggest bird in the world,' she said. 'I found him yesterday, wounded up on the moor, shot to pieces he was – didn't think he'd survive the night. But I brought him back and I nursed him and now he's righter than rain. 'Course he can't fly a lot yet, but he will as soon as he's strong again. He's called Jasper and he's a raven and if you want him on your shoulder it's a penny extra, like the grass snake.'

And then she let them in. His size and his presence overawed and fascinated them totally. He was an immediate success. They could not take their eyes off the enormous black bird that sat glaring down at them from the high hay-rack; and once they had seen him perching on Kate's shoulder everyone wanted a turn – at a penny a time.

The biscuit-tin bank weighed a lot heavier that night. Kate knew now exactly what she would do with the money, but wondered how she could ever save enough.

It was little Laura Linnet's mouse that gave her the idea. The next morning she was taking a handful of purloined minced meat into the stable for Jasper's breakfast when Laura Linnet came running into the yard, her face red and smudged with tears. She had a box in her hands, a brown cardboard box with holes in the top.

'It's my mouse,' she cried. 'The cat was playing with it and I shooed it away but it's hurt and I think maybe it's dead. It's not hardly moving but I thought if you could mend that big black bird then you could mend my mouse.'

By this time all Laura's brothers and sisters and cousins were filling the yard, all of them good zoo customers. They were all watching and waiting for her decision. Kate lifted the lid of the box and saw that the mouse was still living. Its eyes were open and it was lying in one corner of the box its heart beating frantically. Kate's mind was working feverishly for she could see already the opportunities but had yet to work them out. She thought for a full minute, appearing to examine the mouse minutely as a doctor would a patient. Then when her plan was fully formed, she announced to everyone that she could indeed cure it.

'It takes time though,' she said. 'Always does. I'll have to keep the mouse until tomorrow afternoon. By that time it'll be better.'

'How will you do it?' Laura asked, sniffing back her tears.

'I have my ways,' Kate said mysteriously. 'I have my ways. There's not a lot I can't do when I put my mind to it.' And then she added, 'It'll cost you five pence though.'

Miss Marney was not sure if she would ever see Kate again. She had lain awake all night wondering if her secret might have frightened the little girl away, so she was delighted when she saw Kate opening the gate from the moor and running up towards the house; and she was only too pleased to take in the injured mouse for it meant she would be seeing more of her new friend whose company had become suddenly very important to her after all the long years of loneliness.

'Laura's very upset, you know,' said Kate, 'and seeing as how you've got the healing powers, I thought, if you don't mind – I thought maybe you could cure it.'

'Do you know, Kate, I really don't like mice. I don't know why. But I'll do what I can for anything you bring me,' said the old lady setting the box down on the kitchen table and peering anxiously inside. 'But no one must know about it. No one must ever know.' And she poured out a cup of strong sweet tea again and sat down in her rocking-chair smiling happily. 'Do you like stories, Kate?' she said leaning forward. 'Shall I read you a story that no one's ever heard before?' She did not wait for an answer, for she knew she did not need to. 'I've called it "The Giant's Necklace".'

It was a ghostly little story and Kate sat enthralled throughout; but the tea and the story came to an end too soon, as all good things do; and with the promise that she would be back tomorrow to collect the mouse, Kate ran back down past the Eagle's Nest across the road and back home to Wicca.

Kate had absolute faith in Miss Marney's healing powers and so she was not a bit surprised that when she went back to pick up the mouse the next day it was running round its box fully restored. She stayed for her tea and her story, this time a strange one about a crippled boy who went to live with the seals, before she made her way back home with the mouse-box.

Laura Linnet and her friends arrived at the greenhouse soon after she got back and when Kate opened the box there was a gasp of admiration and amazement from everyone around her.

'That'll be five pence,' said Kate, and then she made her announcement. 'I'll be setting up an animal hospital,' she said. 'It'll be in the old chapel – in secret. My powers will only work if it's in secret. And I don't want anyone else ever to know. If they do all the animals I have healed will just roll over and die. Bring along any sick animals, any bird, any creepy-crawly. I'll cure anything you like for five pence a time.'

So Kate Trelochie's financial empire spread from the zoo to a thriving hospital in the old roofless chapel all hung about with ivy and brambles and with ash trees growing up where the altar once stood. Kate would sit on a granite block under the ash trees by the back wall with Jasper on her shoulder, and hold her veterinary court. Several times she had tried to release Jasper who could now fly perfectly well, but he did not seem to want to leave her and she now went everywhere with him permanently attached to her shoulder.

All summer long the children came with their egg-bound hens, their limping dogs and their battle-scarred cats. They brought half-squashed frogs, crushed moles, torn fledglings and even a goldfish that could only swim upside-down and was losing its tail. Kate took them all in and carried them in secret up onto the moor to Miss Marney who would keep them for the night, heal them, and then return them to Kate the next day when she came for her tea and her stories.

Kate spent most of her days now up in the lost house with Miss Marney listening to her strangely compelling tales – about the white horse of Zennor, about the milk-drinking knockers of Tremedda. She explored the house and browsed through the books and she talked endlessly to Miss Marney whom she discovered was becoming increasingly anxious as the summer finally came towards its end. She found she was worrying more about her books than about herself.

'It's the damp,' she said. 'It hurts them, you know,

more than it hurts me. Just so long as my books are dry and I'm a little warm, I'm as happy as a lark and then I can write. All I need is a thick woollen coat and a woolly hat to cover my ears. The worst thing about getting old Kate is that you can't keep warm like you used to. Up to now I've only been able to write in the summer time. You see, I can only write when I'm warm and happy.'

In spite of the success of her animal hospital enterprise, by the autumn Kate had only half the money she needed, and so she came reluctantly to the conclusion that she would have to auction off her zoo. She had nothing else to sell. The zoo was not bringing in much money these days for she had no time now to collect new specimens and everyone had seen the old ones too often. Even the fascination for holding the grass snake was wearing thin. The animals she knew were all replaceable and anyway they would go to good homes. What had to be done, she thought, had to be done.

She held the auction in the ruined chapel and the prices went sky high. Each bid was for a penny so the bidding took some time, but her friends seemed incapable of resisting the temptation to out bid someone else. After all, what was one penny more? Within an hour every creepy-crawly was sold and she had made over five pounds – enough she knew for what she had in mind.

She was just counting her money to be sure, when everyone fell quiet around her. There was the sound of plodding, hesitant hoofbeats and little Laura Linnet came in through the door of the chapel leading her old horse. She had tears pouring down her cheeks.

'The vet's been,' she said, 'and he says Rubin's dying and he wants to shoot him. He wants to shoot my Rubin.'

The horse's head hung almost to the ground and its legs could scarcely carry its weight. He moved slowly into the middle of the chapel and sank heavily to the ground, exhausted.

'I'll pay you anything, Kate,' Laura begged. 'Just help him, please help him. You must help him.'

Kate knelt down by the horse and stroked his neck. He was breathing fast and she could hear a terrible wheezing in the lungs. She could see from the way he sank down that even if she could get him to his feet again she could not walk him all the way to Miss Marney's house on the moor. The faces around her were all expectant, and she knew how popular old Rubin was and that he meant all the world to little Laura Linnet. She stood up slowly.

'I think I can save him,' she said. 'But it will take time – maybe more than just a day – and it will take all my healing powers.' She needed to give herself room for manoeuvre while she thought things out. 'He's very sick,' she said. 'I've never seen a horse as sick as this. He can hardly breathe.'

'But the vet will be back tomorrow morning,' said Laura. 'Father said that unless Rubin looks better by then, he'll have to have him shot. And he will, he will.'

'I'll try,' Kate said finally, but try as she did to disguise it there was little confidence in her voice. 'But I can't promise anything. Go home now all of you and leave me alone with Rubin. I can't work my healing powers with people around me. Go away and remember – not a word to anyone. Meet back here tomorrow first thing.'

They obeyed as they had always done. Kate knew that some of the little ones already thought she was a witch and she used that fear as a threat. Some time ago she had made it known that if any of them betrayed their secret, and told anyone of her healing powers, she had the power to turn them into toads. No one she felt sure would have the courage to put that threat to the test and so her secret was safe.

Kate's mother and father always went to bed early for they had to be up early every morning. She waited fully clothed under her blankets until she heard them stop talking in their bedroom and then crept downstairs. It was a star-bright night with the full moon lighting her way up the tracks towards Miss Marney's house. The first frost of the year glistened on the rocks. She knocked and called out:

'It's me, Miss Marney. Don't worry. It's only me. I need help.'

Over a warm welcome cup of sweet tea in the kitchen she told Miss Marney everything, all about her animal hospital in the chapel. She confessed how she had used her healing powers without ever telling her.

Miss Marney listened in silence, her chair rocking back and forth.

'Old Rubin is dying in the chapel, Miss Marney, and I can't do anything for him,' she went on. 'You must come. I can't get him up here – he's too weak. Miss Marney, you must come – you're the only one who can save him.'

'Is it him you want saved, Kate?' Miss Marney asked, 'or do you want me to save you?'

'Both,' Kate said honestly enough. 'But Rubin's the oldest horse around – nearly forty he is. Everyone knows him. Everyone loves him – we've all ridden him. Please Miss Marney.'

'One thing I still don't understand,' said Miss Marney looking hard at Kate. 'The money. I know you too well Kate – you'd not make money out of the suffering of animals. What did you want the money for? Tell me that Kate.'

Kate could scarcely see the old lady through the tears in her eyes. 'I wanted it to be a surprise,' she said. 'I didn't want to tell you. I just wanted to give it to you for all the tea and the stories and the nice talks we've had.'

'What did you want to give me?' said the old lady leaning forward in her chair and reaching out to take Kate's hand in hers.

'A coat,' Kate said. 'There's a coat I've seen in a shop in Penzance – second-hand shop. But it's warm and woolly and it's only ten pounds and I wanted you to have it for the winter. You said it was the thing you most wanted in the world, so that's why I collected the money – and I've got enough from the zoo and the animal hospital to pay for it and for a woolly hat I've seen as well. They said they'd keep it in the shop for me – I was going to get it next week and then this had to happen.'

The old lady lay back in her chair and smiled. 'You're a kind little person Kate Trelochie,' she said, 'as kind a one as I'll ever meet. I'll do it for Rubin, I'll do it for you and for my warm woolly coat, but I must be back before morning. I don't want to be seen down there with you.'

Kate put her arms around the old lady and hugged her, and then helped her into her corn-sacks and tied them around with cord. With a last sip of warm tea inside them they went out into the frosty night and hurried across the moor hand in hand and down towards the sea that shimmered silver under the white light of the moon. And from Pendeen Lighthouse, the light carved out its arc over the land and the sea, and seemed to wink at them.

Once in the chapel Miss Marney crouched down over the horse and felt him all over. She looked in his mouth and smelt his breath before sitting back on her haunches to consider. Then slowly, so slowly she extended her hands a few inches above his chest.

'I'll be some time, Kate,' she whispered. 'You stay by the door and keep watch. And stay awake mind.'

But Kate used only her ears as watchdogs and looked on as Miss Marney worked. She did not touch Rubin but knelt over him, her hands held out straight like detectors, and always over the horse's chest. The hours passed and all that could be heard was the sound of the sea, the occasional hoot of an owl and Rubin's laboured breathing, and then she saw Miss Marney take off her sacks and lay them over the horse.

'You'll be cold, Miss Marney,' Kate whispered.

'No I won't,' she said, and she lay down beside the horse and put her arms around him. 'I'm tired, I shall sleep for a bit now. Keep a good look-out and wake me before it's light.'

Kate settled down by the chapel wall and pulled her coat up around her ears. To keep awake she tried to count the stones in the chapel wall. Her last thoughts were of the miners who must have come here to pray all those years ago. She wondered what they would think of it now if they came back and found it ruined and deserted.

She woke because she was woken by someone shaking her shoulder. It was little Laura Linnet. The chapel was filled with whispering children who stood, backs to the walls as far away from Miss Marney as they could. Miss Marney herself was pulling on her sacks.

'You dropped off, Kate,' she said, her voice full of fatigue and disappointment. 'That was a shame.'

'It's Mad Miss Marney,' someone said, too loud.

But then Rubin lifted his head from the ground and sat up. He looked around him sleepily, his eyes blinking in the light. He got to his feet easily enough, nuzzled Miss Marney gently and began to pull at the grass beside her.

'Mad I may be,' she said. 'But your horse is better. Keep him warm and well fed and he'll be all right. He'll go on for more years than I will.'

And she hobbled out of the chapel past Kate who was too sleepy to find the words to stop her.

Kate confessed the whole deception to her friends and offered them their money back. Not one of them would take it – indeed it was Laura Linnet herself who suggested they should all go up to the lost house that afternoon after Kate had bought the coat.

And so a cavalcade of children and dogs and cats and horses and creepy-crawlies in boxes made their way that same afternoon up the black track over the moor to Miss Marney's house. Kate brought with her the bright red woollen coat with a fur collar, and a warm white bobble-hat for Miss Marney's ears. She did not come out at first when Kate knocked. The children all fell silent and listened. They could hear her talking away to herself. Kate knocked again.

'Come in Kate,' Miss Marney called, and they all trooped into the house through the book-lined living room and into the kitchen.

'I've brought your coat Miss Marney,' she said, 'I've come to say sorry, and we've all come to say thank you. We've told everyone about how kind you are to animals and about how you heal them and we've told everyone at home you're not a bit mad or witchy. Everyone knows you're a healer now, Miss Marney – the vet says it was a miracle. And my father says he'll be calling on you when his animals get sick. There'll be money enough to keep your books dry.'

Miss Marney smiled. 'They say,' she said slowly, 'they say that everything is for the best in the world. But I never believed it, not until now.'

And she took the coat and tried it on.

'It's a bit on the large side,' she said standing swathed in pillar-box red from head to toe. 'But it'll keep me all the warmer. And I like the hat, but I won't put it on now because it'll spoil my hair. Now, children, will you all have some tea? I've only one cup so you'll have to have a sip and pass it around. And if you'll find a place to sit down I'll tell you one of my stories. Some people think I talk to myself I know, but I don't – well not often. I tell myself my stories out aloud before I write them down. I haven't yet had time to put this one on paper. It's all about an old lady they once called Mad Miss Marney.'

EGMONT PRESS: ETHICAL PUBLISHING

Egmont Press is about turning writers into successful authors and children into passionate readers – producing books that enrich and entertain. As a responsible children's publisher, we go even further, considering the world in which our consumers are growing up.

Safety First
Naturally, all of our books meet legal safety requirements. But we go further than this; every book with play value is tested to the highest standards – if it fails, it's back to the drawing-board.

Made Fairly
We are working to ensure that the workers involved in our supply chain – the people that make our books – are treated with fairness and respect.

Responsible Forestry
We are committed to ensuring all our papers come from environmentally and socially responsible forest sources.

For more information, please visit our website at www.egmont.co.uk/ethical

Mixed Sources
Product group from well-managed forests and other controlled sources
www.fsc.org Cert no. TT-COC-002332
© 1996 Forest Stewardship Council

Egmont is passionate about helping to preserve the world's remaining ancient forests. We only use paper from legal and sustainable forest sources, so we know where every single tree comes from that goes into every paper that makes up every book.

This book is made from paper certified by the Forestry Stewardship Council (FSC), an organisation dedicated to promoting responsible management of forest resources. For more information on the FSC, please visit **www.fsc.org**. To learn more about Egmont's sustainable paper policy, please visit **www.egmont.co.uk/ethical**.